## It was the aftershocks that really shook her world...

"Cane, we can't make love again," Bernadette murmured.

Cane's brows rose and the light went out of his eyes. "No? Why not?"

"Because it's not right. Not if we're working together."

"Let me get this straight. You're saying that as long as we're living together and working together, we can't make love?"

She wasn't sure why, but she decided she'd better stick to her guns. "Something like that."

"You mean, if I go back to my crowded apartment with two friends, where I don't have a bed or a bath, you'll let me back in your bed again?"

"It wouldn't be a business partnership then."

"Okay." He turned around and headed toward the door.

"Where are you going?" she asked, suddenly sorry for her own decision.

He gave her a smoldering look over his shoulder and said, "I'm moving out."

Dear Reader,

All men are not created equal. Some are rough around the edges. Tough-minded but tenderhearted. Incredibly sexy. The tempting fulfillment of every woman's fantasy. These are Temptation's Rebels & Rogues.

Now meet top author Rita Clay Estrada's Hurricane Mitchell—a sexy rogue if ever there was one. Rita is the award-winning author of 16 emotionally involving, totally satisfying Temptations. She lives and works in Texas, land of the ultimate cowboy hero.

Look for a new Rebels & Rogues story in April 1996. Superromance author Patricia Keelyn makes her Temptation debut with #582 *Nobody's Hero*.

Happy Reading!

Birgit Davis-Todd
Senior Editor, Harlequin Temptation

# Rita Clay Estrada
# THE STORMCHASER

## Harlequin Books

TORONTO • NEW YORK • LONDON
AMSTERDAM • PARIS • SYDNEY • HAMBURG
STOCKHOLM • ATHENS • TOKYO • MILAN
MADRID • WARSAW • BUDAPEST • AUCKLAND

ISBN 0-373-25673-6

THE STORMCHASER

# 1

CANE MITCHELL ENTERED the empty apartment and felt a welcome draft of air-conditioned breeze wash over his heated skin. He'd been working just north of Los Angeles in the San Gabriel Mountains, which generally provided a cool respite from sun-baked L.A. in the summer. But the heat had been as bad there as it was on the dry, desert floor of the coast.

He dropped his portable file box by the kitchen bar and pushed the button on the answering machine. No personal messages for him or his two roommates. Just questions from insureds concerning their claims.

More work. *Great!* Just what a burned-out insurance adjuster needed.

He continued to listen and jot down names and numbers as the answering machine spewed out what felt like a never-ending stream of messages. He glanced at the memo pad beside the phone. He would read the other messages later. Strolling into Reed's bathroom, he stripped, still half listening to the tape.

When he heard his name whispered by a woman with a low sultry voice, he stopped to listen carefully to her words.

"Mr. Cane Mitchell, my name is Bernadette Conrad and my insurance agent told me you are my adjuster.

My house is yellow-tagged, so I only have restricted access to it. Right now I'm staying at my son's apartment while I wait for you to get to my case. Can you call me here and let me know how long it will be before you can assess the damage? Since my business was in my home, I'm really stuck."

She left her phone number, said thank-you, and hung up.

Her melodious voice rang in his ears.

Cane had in fact tried to get a hold of Bernadette Conrad several times, calling every morning and night. He'd even gone by her home and left a note with his name and phone number. Hadn't she been there to see it?

"Damn," he muttered, stepping into the shower to wash off the day's hard work. He'd walked on three roofs, crawled under two pier-and-beam homes and experienced one rumbling aftershock. If that damn earthquake hadn't caused enough damage and injury, the severe aftershocks were putting the final blows to numerous houses and buildings.

As the hot spray pounded his sore muscles, he deliberately blocked out all but the most superficial thoughts and concentrated on the feel of the pulsing stream of water. He deserved a few minutes of not thinking about anything—especially work.

By the time his roommates returned to the apartment Cane had almost finished cooking dinner for them all.

Cassandra arrived first, looking thoroughly wilted by the heat. "I thought California was supposed to have wonderful weather," she complained, running a hand through blond hair turned dark by the misty rain that had fallen continuously all day long. "I feel more like a limp rag here than in the humid heat of Houston," she said wearily.

"Tell me," he replied with a grin. He'd felt the same way before his shower. "Get changed and have some dinner. It'll make you feel better before you have to hit the computer."

"Oh, whee." Her voice was a tired, dry monotone.

"Ain't life wonderful?" Reed agreed as he stepped into the apartment hearing the last of his sister's comments. "Something smells great. That means Cane is cooking, thank the Lord."

"Get smart, brother, and I'll place a wet and muddy Reebok on your rear end," Cassandra threatened before disappearing into her room and shutting the door behind her.

Reed looked after her, then over at Cane and sniffed. "Beef Stroganoff?"

"Enchiladas with Swiss cheese and kale," Cane corrected, basting the enchiladas with a deep red sauce. "Your nose is confusing cream with Swiss cheese."

"My nose never was up to snuff." Reed grinned. "I still can't identify a woman by the kind of perfume she wears."

Cane grabbed several plates from the kitchen cabinet and set them next to the covered skillet on the stove. "That's because you like all women. Plural."

"And I can't see why you don't," his best friend said. "I don't understand how anyone would rather be with a bunch of guys in a pool hall, when they could be holding a woman in their arms."

"Except for Cass, they're too much trouble."

"Isn't it great?" Reed reached into the refrigerator for a beer, popped the cap and poured it into a glass because his sister would complain if she caught him drinking from the bottle. "I see woman trouble coming at me and I grin from ear to ear. Eureka, let the good times roll."

"How about the bad times? Without women, men wouldn't be in constant turmoil." Cane took a beer from the fridge and drank it from the bottle. He didn't care that Cass didn't like the habit. She wasn't his sister.

Cane wiped the beer foam from his lips with the back of his hand. "I'd bet my last dollar you've got a date tonight. Some babe you met today. You seem to meet a new woman at every natural disaster."

Reed grinned. "No, I don't, but I'm meeting her tomorrow night for a glass of wine. She was in the restaurant where I stopped to have lunch."

Cass came in from the front bedroom, a terry cloth robe tied around her tall slim body and a towel wrapped around her blond hair. "You're a regular Casanova."

"I've always been partial to women's company, so I make it my business to find out what women like, and then I try to give it to them."

"No kidding," Cane mocked. "Now, why didn't I think of that approach?"

"Because you don't have to. Woman fall at your feet," Cass explained, a note of disgust in her voice. "The difference is that Reed gets emotionally involved with every woman he likes, and you, my *dear* Cane, won't let any woman near your emotions."

"Thank you for your diagnosis," Reed said, mockingly. "If we are the representatives of our sex, are you spokesperson for yours?"

"Not hardly." Cass gave a sniff. "It's hard to believe my own sex would go so gaga over two such obviously deficient men, but it's a fact. Though it's beyond me why."

Both men laughed.

"You don't know what you're missing, Cane, keeping yourself at such a distance. A woman in your life might make you happy. Can you imagine that?"

"What about the stress, the heartache? In case you haven't noticed, the stress factor in this job is pretty strong. We're always in the middle of some disaster. That doesn't bring out the best in people."

"I know, but being with someone might make it a lot more pleasurable to bear," she said.

"No, thanks, love. I plan to stay footloose and fancy-free."

She gave a delicate humph, then grabbed a plate and speared an enchilada.

Cane had known Cass since she was entering high school, and had always had a soft spot for her. Reed was lucky to have had a terrific family to grow up in. Some people weren't so fortunate....

The three sat on the floor around the coffee table, sharing a loaf of French bread with Cane's dinner and commiserating over the aches and pains of the day.

Cane enjoyed this daily ritual as much as he enjoyed his work. Being an insurance adjuster who specialized in natural disasters wasn't an easy job, but as Cass said, someone had to do it. The truth was, they all enjoyed being adjusters, and the traveling around the country their work involved. Although they loved their hometown of Houston, it was nice to travel.

Cane and Reed had originally taken the furnished corporate apartment in L.A. together to save money by sharing rent and office equipment. Then, when Cass got her commercial adjuster's license and begged to join them, they fitted her into their setup. After all, this was her first "disaster," and they wanted to be sure she had someone watching over her.

Since it was only a two-bedroom apartment, Cane had given Cass his room. He shared Reed's bathroom but slept on the couch because he needed less sleep than the other two and was usually the last to bed and the first one out the door in the morning.

After dinner, Reed and Cass went back to work.

With a heavy sigh, Cane looked at them both and knew it was time for him to do the same. Then he remembered the low, melodious voice of a woman so saddened by her loss.

Taking the cellular phone out to the patio, he sat under the awning, his legs propped on the balcony, and read through the information he had on the insured. There were two names on the loss notice—hers and her husband's. Bernadette Conrad had an excellent policy, with a minimal deduction; most of her home and contents were covered.

Cane dialed her number.

"Mrs. Conrad?"

"Ms.," the melodious voice corrected firmly. "And yes, this is she."

Another feminist. "Sorry," he said slowly. "I'm Cane Mitchell, your insurance adjuster for Home Insurance Company. I received your message today. I've been trying to get in touch with you for the past two weeks."

"I just found out, Mr. Mitchell. My neighbor went into my house and brought out the tape in my answering machine. I'm sorry. I thought my insurance agent had let you know where I was."

"That's fine," Cane soothed. "I would have gotten a hold of you eventually. Can I make an appointment with you or your husband to come out and scope the property for damage?"

"That property is mine. There is no husband and hasn't been for over seven years," she said sharply. Cane wondered if there was a little tension between her and her ex.

"I seem to be apologizing all over the place tonight. I'm sorry, Ms. Conrad, but the sheet of information the insurance company gave me on you has your ex-husband listed. That's something you might want to take up with your insurance agent."

She sighed heavily. "I didn't mean to attack you, Mr. Mitchell. But, I've lost my sense of humor with these aftershocks lately. Once I have my house back in order and can open my business again, maybe I'll regain my easygoing attitude."

"Maybe," he conceded, but he doubted it. "Can we make an appointment for me to see your property?"

"My business is gone, and so is my house. I'm fast running out of both money and credit. I'll take your first available time."

Something in her voice tugged at him and Cane knew he was a goner. No matter how hard he tried, the woman's problems affected him. "Okay," he said gruffly. "I can be there tomorrow afternoon around three."

"Wonderful. I'll meet you there," she said, her relief evident.

"It will take approximately three hours or more to do a complete scope," he warned.

"I'll be there," she said simply. "With no home and no job, what else do I have to do?"

"You've got a choice, Ms. Conrad. All this will happen whether you smile or not. You might as well smile."

Cane clicked off the phone and stared out at the ribbon of car lights on the Ventura Freeway—the last of the evening traffic racing home to friends and loved ones. Watching it underlined his aloneness.

Everyone had somebody special in their life. For one of those rare times, he felt lonely. He was going to be forty years old in two months, and there was no one who wanted to be with him forever and love him for all his moods and ways. In fact, he no longer believed in the kind of love singers crooned about and writers waxed sentimental over. His six-year marriage had failed. But to be honest, there had been more lust than love in their relationship from the beginning. How many happy relationships and marriages were there, really? He could count the ones he knew of, on one hand. Most of the time, he was okay with being alone. Besides, he'd been alone so long, he'd gotten half used to it. It was hard to imagine living with a woman on a "forever" basis. As if he still believed in "happily ever after."

Cane shook off the feeling of loneliness, he stood and stretched. It was time to get to work. Tomorrow was another day—and one that would be interesting if only because he could put a body to the lovely voice of Bernadette Conrad.

Why was he so curious about her? He was a confirmed loner. It must be her voice, he told himself. Sexy. Assured yet vulnerable. There was something enticing about the way she sounded. What was his problem? He was getting carried away. She probably was an elderly chunkette with bunions—given his luck lately.

CALIFORNIA DECIDED to show Cane just how perfect its weather could be. The sun shone gently, warming his skin; a light, refreshing breeze caressed him.

With the windows open on his shiny black GMC truck, Cane pushed through traffic toward Bernadette Conrad's house—or what was left of it.

By the time he reached her street, he wished he'd made the appointment for sometime next week instead of this afternoon. He didn't like late-afternoon calls. He wanted to get back to the apartment before the freeway was transformed into the world's largest parking lot and he was breathing high-octane exhaust.

While he groused to himself about falling into the helping-the-damsel-in-distress trap, he spied the numbers on the mailbox and pulled to the curb. It was an unusual house, painted two shades of tan with crisp forest-green shutters and doors. The garage faced the street, and a long wooden pathway led to the front door, which was much farther back and protected by an ornamental wrought-iron gate. What made the property distinctive was that it was built over a gully, and the covered wooden-walkway and garden below were the only links to the garage and house.

He checked out the garage, and was unable to see any damage from the front. Even the driveway didn't seem to have more than the usual cracks or dips. He looked in the direction of the deck walk.

A slim young woman with thick, dark hair pulled into a ponytail sat just inside the yellow-tagged wrought-iron gate. Dressed in a long, loose-fitting, gauzy print dress, she was perched on a cut log obviously meant to hold the trailing plant she cradled in her lap. She hadn't seen him yet. Her gaze was still locked on the plant, as she meticulously picked off rotting leaves and dropped them, one by one, into the ravine below.

She was concentrating on the plant so intensely that Cane bet she was forcing herself to do so, so she couldn't pay attention to anything else. He'd seen that syndrome before. Unless he was way off base, this was one very upset lady.

"Miss Conrad?" he called, as he reached the middle of the walkway.

Startled, she looked up. Slowly her look of tension dissipated to be replaced by one of the saddest smiles Cane had ever seen. She stood, set the plant back on the log and brushed her hands together to dust off the loose soil. "Yes. Mr. Mitchell?" she asked, before reaching for the gate handle on her side.

"Yes, I am," he replied easily, standing a few feet away from the swing door. He waited for her to unlock the gate and let him in. "See?" he stated teasingly as he pointed to the red insignia over his left shirt pocket that proclaimed him a member of the catastrophe team for his insurance company. There was still hesitation in her wide, hazel-eyed gaze, so he reached into the pocket and pulled out a card, then handed it to her through the wrought iron.

Ms. Conrad glanced warily at the card, then back at him.

"Now, ma'am," Cane said slowly, letting his thick East Texas accent flow through his words, hoping it would disarm her a little. It had worked before on other insureds. "I understand that you're as wary as a long-tailed cat at a young boy's birthday party, but I suggest you let me in to do my job or call the cat office so they can confirm who I am. Otherwise we're at what we call a Mexican standoff and neither of us gets what we want."

"Cat office?"

"Catastrophe office," he explained with a smile. "Where the claims are processed."

Her shoulders relaxed. "I'm sorry," she murmured, unlocking the gate and allowing him entrance. "I'm afraid I haven't adapted as well to the tremors as I should have."

"I didn't know anyone had, ma'am." Cane spoke in a low, easy tone. "Many haven't been able to adjust yet. Can't say I blame them, either. These aftershocks don't give a warning. It's not anything like a hurricane, tornado or flood, where you know one is coming or at least have a weather warning. These damn—pardon me, ma'am—darn things just shake the earth when you least expect them to."

"I hate them," she said, her voice so low he almost didn't hear her.

Her gaze didn't meet his. Instead she turned and led the way along the deck, her slim back swaying slightly with each step. "Let me show you my home, Mr. Mitchell."

Bernadette Conrad was a very classy, very feminine lady, Cane thought appreciatively, as he followed the gentle undulation of her hips.

"I used to have a foster mother whose name was Bernadette. She was a lovely woman. Only we used to call her Bette." He gave that piece of information to make conversation, and perhaps relax her. It didn't seem to work.

"I don't care for nicknames much," was all she said as she opened the front door and led him inside. He stopped to glance at the door's stress points, then entered, stepping directly onto the polished white-pine floors of the spacious living and dining area. Peach and cream walls were a backdrop for the many framed oils and watercolors in all sizes and shapes. But right now the pictures were all at an angle, dangling from dancing wire. It looked as if a drunken sailor had hung them.

Her gaze followed his. "I straighten them every time I come over. When I return it's a reminder of how much the earth has shaken since I left."

She looked around. "This used to be my haven from the world, Mr. Mitchell. I used to come home and believe I was safe from everything here. Now it's a disaster area and I'm afraid of being in my own house for very long. I'm afraid it could hurt me."

Her pain was visible. Cane couldn't think of a thing to say. Instead, he nodded and continued to look around. Every wall showed deep stress cracks, especially around the windows and doorways. Slashing the far outside wall was a tear scored so deep into the stucco, he knew there was structural damage.

Cane walked over to the gash to examine it. The white-pine floor had bowed up and he felt as if he was actually climbing to the wall. Reaching into a small pack on his hip, he pulled out his camera and began shooting the slash marks, then backed up and took a few shots of the dented and scraped floor.

"There's more," she said after he'd completed his inspection of the gash.

"I'm sure there is. You don't get a yellow tag on your house without some pretty extensive damage."

Despite her nervousness, he continued taking measurements and photos, then entered the next room and began the process again. When the inspection of the first floor was completed, they headed upstairs to the bedrooms.

A beautiful Oriental, cream-and-green carpet covered most of the floor in the master bedroom; most of the pine furniture was overturned. He stepped gingerly around the broken glass scattered all over the carpet from the shattered windows.

"Where were you when it struck?"

"Right there," she said, her voice strained. She pointed to a pillow, just inches from the brass lamp. "The quake literally shook me out of bed. Thank goodness it shook me the right way or I'd have been hit on the head."

He stared at the pillow and realized just how close she had come to death. The heavy lamp would certainly have caused damage. He imagined her lovely head bleeding— He cut off that mental image and brought himself back to the job at hand. He'd done adjusting long enough to know that he couldn't get emotionally involved.

A funny feeling in the pit of his stomach told him the room and the woman were affecting him more than was safe. It was hard to separate her from the room. It was a place for making love, for proclaiming love; a room where a woman and a man would tell each other their most intimate secrets. He brushed the image aside. This wasn't the time to let a fantasy take over, he told himself. Instead, he busied himself with measuring the room.

Finally he spoke. "Great room. Did you put it together or copy it from some magazine?"

"I put it together," she said softly, looking around as if her gaze was a caress on every piece of wood and fabric in the room. "It was a labor of love. I don't think I'll get tired of it for a long while to come."

Cane wrote down the measurements on his clipboard. "Where'd you get the idea for it?"

"From several places. But most of all . . ." Her voice dwindled away.

"Most of all?" he prompted when she didn't finish her answer.

"Most of all, from my heart." Her chin tilted up defiantly as if to tell him she wouldn't take his laughing

about this area of her life. It looked like it was something out of a fantasy, and he'd just bet the fantasy was
all hers.

That was all right. Who was he to talk? Everybody
had fantasies. Even he did. Especially right this minute. "Well, ma'am," he drawled. "If it had been me, I'd
have decorated the whole house in this style."

Her beautiful eyes widened. "Really?"

"Really."

"My son thinks it looks like something out of a
woman's fantasy."

He felt a wave of jealousy flow over him and he had
to push it away quickly. "How old is your son?"

"Almost nineteen."

"What do eighteen-year-old boys know?" he joked.

Her smile was his reward.

Walking into the next room, he stopped in the center
of what had to be her son's bedroom. It was filled with
plaques and posters of hockey heroes—some signed,
some obviously kept just for the fun of it. "A hockey
fanatic. The kid has potential."

Her laughter was delightful. Some of the strain of
being in her beloved house was easing. She must have
been like this before the quake—before her world
turned upside down. "He knows hockey, all right," she
said. "He and his father used to keep up with each and
every player and team."

"Your husband must have a lot of time on his hands."
Cane hadn't meant to sound so mean-spirited—it just
came out that way.

"My husband died in an auto accident seven years ago, Mr. Mitchell. He was only thirty-one years old."

Damn. That was tough. "I'm sorry, Mrs. Conrad. I didn't know."

"Ms."

"Ms." Her voice had a definiteness about it.

He stared over at her. She looked vulnerable, sophisticated and . . . terrific. "Why the Ms. instead of Mrs.?"

She sighed heavily, reminded of another tragedy. He could have kicked himself for bringing it up. "I was Mrs. until a few years after my husband died, when I realized there was a difference between being married and having a man to protect you in a man's world and being a widow and having no one to protect you in the real world."

"Oh, come on, now," Cane began.

But she ignored his attempt to dissuade her. "The Ms. means that whether I have a man in my life or not, I deal with my own problems and make my own solutions. It works for me instead of against me."

"No offense, ma'am, but how could being a Mrs. work against you? Why, being a wife is a full-time job, just like mine is." He smiled charmingly. "Especially if there're children."

"Being a wife means that mechanics and plumbers and electricians expect your husband to handle the problem of checking their work. It's not always done correctly by some of the less honest. Problem is, if you've never had to deal with a company before and you don't have a husband, you might not know their reputation. In that case, get a hold of a bad apple, and that repairman will help separate the 'little woman' from her money."

Cane looked at her for a moment, transfixed by the movement of her mouth more than the outpouring of her words. She had a beautiful mouth—full lips that tilted up slightly at the corners. "Well, I'll be," he murmured before turning and entering the next bedroom cum office. A copier, computer, and fax machine were piled in a broken heap on the floor. He guessed several thousand dollars' worth of equipment had been totaled here.

"I could barely lift that copier," Bernadette said softly as she pointed to the other end of the room. Her voice quaked slightly. "Yet the earth trembled enough to dump that heavy machine to the ground and bounce it across the room."

He heard her fear and tried to ignore it by talking about everyday things. "Do you also have business insurance?" he asked, looking down at the Loss notice to find the insurance rider codes.

"Yes. It's all covered. A few pieces were also under warranty with the manufacturer. I'll have those replaced in another week or so, when the store finally gets them in."

Cane continued to measure and write. He measured the length of a gash running from ceiling to floor. Interior damage was greatest in this corner of the house. "Must have come from this direction."

"I didn't know earthquakes had directions."

"Just like a water wave coming to shore, it will usually broadside one area of the house before striking the rest," Cane replied. "That's why some china cabinets are shaken from front to back and fall down, while others are swayed from side to side and not one piece of glass will be broken."

He looked over at her, wishing there was something he could say that would take away some of the pain. There was nothing. "I need to take measurements outside, now," he finally said.

"Oh, yes, of course." She turned and led the way down the stairs and to the backyard. He followed again, enjoying the sway of her hips.

The yard was jigsawed in slate, with bright pockets of flowers here and there. The retainer walls enclosing the back portion of the yard had been torn apart—cinder blocks strewn about like blocks thrown by a giant baby.

The grounds were a mess of uprooted plants, broken fencing, splintered timbers, and pots scattered here and there, far from their original resting places. But he could tell that it had been a peaceful place.

Cane looked back at the house and saw the wall that had been gouged in the living room and the office. Even from the outside, he could see the entire wall was bowed from the interior.

"How long ago did they put the yellow tag on your house?"

"Three days after the quake."

"Were you staying here up till then?"

"No. I've been at my son's."

"Will I be able to reach you there, Ms. Conrad?"

"No. I'll be out by next week, when his third room-mate returns. It will be too crowded, so I have to find a place to stay, and a job. I lost my business—my home. Everything." She said the words without emotion, but the look in her eyes told the real story. She was mourning for more than her home and business; she was grieving for her lost way of life. He didn't blame her.

"What kind of business?"

"Six months before the quake, I opened up my own secretarial business. It was something I'd always wanted to do and had finally saved enough to buy all the state-of-the-art equipment I needed. I'd even set up some answering-service lines."

She stopped and swallowed and he felt an overwhelming urge to pat her back and tell her everything was all right. But he knew better.

"Was it a success?"

"More than I had imagined it would be. But now..." Her words trailed off, tears shimmered. Then she gave a light gasp and her hazel eyes widened.

At first, Cane thought she'd seen something. Then he felt the rumble, too. It started like a vibration under his feet, then got progressively stronger. A good-size aftershock was building. He took her arm and led her to the doorway, making sure they were both under it for safety's sake.

Her face became pale and she clenched her hands into fists. "Oh, dear God. No," she whispered.

Every windowpane and door began to shake. The sound grew stronger, turning into a deep growl. Everything in the house clanked and banged. Cane didn't stop to consider what he was doing. Without a moment's hesitation, he took her in his arms and held her, his low voice soothing her. "It's okay. It's just an aftershock. It's okay."

But her body began shaking against his body as much as the earth quaked under his feet. The vibration became stronger. All the windows and doors in the house began rattling as if ready to fall out of their casings.

Once he realized that the aftershock was as intense as it was going to get, he relaxed. Instead, he focused on the shaking woman in his arms who was sobbing as if her heart had broken.

"I can't stand it," she choked. "I don't know what to do."

"I do." He continued holding her for a moment, relishing the contact. She was warm and soft and so very sweet. Her perfume wafted up, filling his lungs with a light, airy scent.

"That was just a baby quake. Nothing to it." His right hand stroked her back in a comforting fashion. "It's over. It's over."

"For now," she said, her voice muffled against his chest. "But it's not the end of them, is it?"

"No, but it won't be as bad as the first one." He tried to soothe her, but he knew his words were empty. He wasn't in charge of natural disasters—not this week, anyway. Hell, at this point he wasn't in charge of his own body's reactions.

Bernadette gave a laugh, pulling her head away from his chest and looking at him with eyes that shone with unshed tears. "Promise?"

He didn't miss a beat. "Yes, ma'am. Cross my heart and hope to die."

She smiled and warning bells rang loudly in his head. But not loud enough to drown out her next words.

"Now, what do I do? Fear earthquakes for the rest of my life? That's hard to do in this part of the country. I'm so tired of staying with my son in an apartment. But even in this state, I know I certainly can't live in a house that's threatening to fall in on my head."

Now he was on steadier ground. He knew this path of conversation and felt safe with it. Once more he slipped into his professional persona. "First things first. Check into a hotel room and get a good night's sleep. Then, tomorrow, find an earthquake-proof apartment and fax me the contract. Your policy will pay for the removal of furniture and the rental while your home is being repaired."

She looked at him through tear-shined eyes that tugged at his heart as nothing else had in a very long time. "Are you sure?"

"I'm sure. Do it right away. I'll help by setting up whatever I can. Then, once you're out of here, find a contractor to give you a bid on the repairs, write down a complete list of contents that were destroyed or are in need of repair, and start to get your home and business back to normal."

"I've already tried." She rested her forehead against his chest. He wouldn't have moved if another five earthquakes hit. It felt too damn good. She felt so damn sexy.... "No contractor seems to have the time to do anything, much less give a bid. There are too many other damaged homes for them to repair. And I'm so tired of trying. I think I've spoken to everyone having anything to do with construction in the local phone book."

Cane wanted to hold her close again, and that was a sign that it was emotionally unsafe to continue this contact. He dropped his hands from her slim waist and took several steps back. It wasn't easy to keep his distance from the woman he'd just held in his arms, but it was essential. "Don't worry about that. I have several reputable names you can call and determine which you want to work with. Meanwhile, get an apartment you will feel safe in."

She gave a tremulous smile. It was worth the wait. "Thank you, Mr. Mitchell."

She sounded so relieved, as if he'd taken a burden off her shoulders—and somehow he knew he'd placed it directly on his own.

No fool like a Texas fool, he told himself. But it was too late. He had just volunteered to allow Ms. Bernadette Conrad to be his responsibility.

It should have felt a whole lot worse than it did, and that worried Cane more than anything else.

# 2

WITH HANDS THAT WERE still shaking with fear from the aftershock, Bernadette locked the walkway gate leading from her once-beautiful home and slipped behind the wheel of her Cutlass. It took a minute to find enough energy to turn the key, pull into traffic and head back to her son Ian's apartment.

Cane Mitchell had spoken to her for almost half an hour after the tremor, calming her fears. He seemed to understand just how she felt, and that alone made her feel better. She knew he was right. She needed to get a hotel room so she could have some privacy and catch up on her sleep. Living with a couple of college students was too hard on her already shattered nerves. Once she got a place to stay, then she'd contact the structural engineer Cane had recommended to arrange for the necessary repairs to her house.

She wished her best friends were here to help her through this time, but Beth and Sandra had left California. In the past six months, Beth had transferred to New York State, while Sandra had moved to Nevada. Bernadette spoke to them both often on the phone. That was something, but she needed more support.

If structural damage to the house was extensive, she would have to find an apartment to live in until the restoration was completed. However, if the repairs needed were only minimal, she could possibly move back in soon.

But she knew the chance of the damage being minimal was next to nil. When the county inspector had placed the tag on her front door, he had explained some of the damage. The pier-and-beam construction that supported her house had been severely compromised. It would take more than a few structural Band-Aids to fix the problem.

Seeing the damage again made her relive that early morning of terror. She'd been sleeping soundly. At first the quake had felt like a part of her dream—but not for long. It wasn't a rolling quake like all the others she'd experienced. Instead, it jerked and tossed, pitching her out of her own bed. That had turned out to be a blessing, because her brand-new torchère fell across the pillows where she'd been sleeping. The crystal shade had shattered all over her new linens. The earth had literally groaned aloud. Forcing herself to keep her wits about her, she had picked her way to the kitchen and turned off the gas. The phone had rung but she couldn't find it in time to hear her son's voice on her answering machine telling her he was all right.

She'd joined the neighbors outside, and talked, laughed, worried and shared their friendship until after dawn. It wasn't until she was alone again that she realized how short life could be. Had her bed not had a footboard, the dresser would have crushed her. Had she not been tossed out of bed, the lamp might have smashed her skull. Had she not had the forethought to turn off the gas right away, she could have blown up the house. Had she . . .

She blinked back the tears that never seemed to be very far away these days, and got onto the freeway, heading for her son's apartment, adjacent to the University of California.

She had told herself that everything would fall back into place, but life hadn't gone back to normal in a day or so—or even a week or so. The earthquake had changed everything, especially her general outlook and feeling of personal safety.

She and her husband, Nick, had bought this home together after several years of scrimping and saving. At that time, their son, Ian, was just a little guy starting first grade. They had been so proud of all they'd accomplished then.

They were on the verge of a new life, a better life. They were young and full of high hopes that would sustain them into old age.

They'd also been so in love. Nick had been her best friend and lover, just the way romance novels said it should be. And then Nick had died in an auto accident one morning while commuting to work. She'd barely had a chance to say goodbye to him in the flurry of getting everything organized for the day. All she'd had time to give Nick was a quick peck on the cheek and a reminder to call for a dental appointment. An average morning . . .

Ian had yet to be dropped off at school. Her part-time job representing a greeting card company catering to small gift stores had called her to work earlier than usual. There was still so much to do....

Half an hour later, just as she was rushing out the door, she'd received the call from the hospital asking her to come and identify Nick. It couldn't be. She assured them they'd made a mistake, some bizarre error. The Los Angeles area was one of the three largest cities in the United States. There had to be another Nick Conrad living in the area. Didn't they understand? It was not her Nick!

Her Nick. Her childhood friend, adolescent conspirator and teenage lover. They'd dated since they were freshmen in high school, had married two days after graduation and become parents five years later. She'd thought they would be together forever. She'd naively believed that he would be there to weather all her storms, help her through everything in life.

She'd had no time to say goodbye. She'd had no time to ease into the idea of coping alone. She couldn't ask him practical questions, like where their bills were kept and what insurance policies they had. Like which plumber was best and should she take the car to the auto mechanic on the corner or the one down the street. And she couldn't question him on how best to raise their son.

She'd had no time to explain to him that she didn't want to be alone—she wanted to be with him!

But most of all, she hadn't had the chance to tell him how much she loved and needed him and how much she wanted to hear that he loved her and had complete faith that she was capable of carrying on alone.

The traffic accident had snuffed out his breath in less than a minute. And it had changed her whole life and her son's life. A mortgage-insurance policy paid off the house, and another small policy had provided her with an extra little something to live on for a while.

She'd had to grow up fast. It hadn't been easy and it wasn't over yet, but she'd come an enormous way from the lost young woman she'd been then, to the organized, "together" and competent woman she felt she was now.

Until the earthquake.

Just when she thought she'd come so far and was feeling great about her accomplishments.

She had already learned how to pay bills, get and keep a responsible job that paid decently, deal with the world on an equal level. She'd been a single parent who had given her all to her only child.

She'd also worked through the grief and anger over Nick's death and gone on with her life. She'd even started dating. It had been sporadic and unfulfilling and had finally ceased for lack of candidates with potential. No one wanted someone with a child—a woman who barely scraped by, a woman who was still haunted by memories of her dead husband.

Instead, she'd found girlfriends to exchange gossip and have fun and discussions with. It wasn't the same but it was safer.

She still fantasized about finding someone special, especially late in the evening after an exhausting day of work and a trying time with a teenager who thought the world owed him something because it had taken away his dad. At night she occasionally dreamed of making love with a tender lover. In the morning, she inevitably felt even more lonely.

The best cure had been to keep busy. Bernadette lost herself in the two things that gave her the most feedback: her son and her work as a law clerk.

Then, to supplement her income, she began doing odd jobs for others outside the law office where she worked. It started as a way to earn extra money for all those things kids needed, like extra equipment for T-ball or football or hockey or whatever other sport caught her son's fancy.

Two things happened. One, she found she enjoyed working for herself during hours when her son was asleep and the house was quiet. Two, she began getting requests for more work than she could do part-time. That was when the dream of running her own secretarial business was born. She began to save part of the money she earned so she could eventually realize that dream. It was several years before she'd saved enough to buy the necessary equipment and also pay her living expenses for the first six months.

Then, just when Bernadette thought she had the world by the horns, the world bit back with an earthquake. Her emotions, usually so steady, were now always in an uproar. Her calm demeanor had been shattered, leaving someone who resembled her but acted vulnerable and shaky in everyday situations.

At least she hadn't followed her instincts and dropped her earthquake insurance. She'd talked to her insurance agent several times and each time the woman had talked her out of it for another year. Now Bernadette wanted to thank her for it. Having insurance was the only thing that made all this chaos bearable. Because of it, she would be able to repair what had once been her dream home.

Then, once the house was restored, come hell or high water she was moving out of earthquake country. She wasn't sure where she'd go, but she knew it was time to leave California. If she was going to start over, then she'd do it where the earth didn't move under her feet.

If she didn't feel there was a way out of her current situation, she wouldn't be able to cope at all. The thought of leaving was her only hope.

Bernadette parked in her son's apartment-complex lot, which was crowded with much newer cars than hers. Slipping from the driver's seat, she wondered where today's kids got the money to afford those new cars? Parents? A fast-food restaurant job? No wonder Ian thought he was underprivileged—half the cars here were foreign, and a third of those German imports. Amazing.

Pasting a smile on her lips, she headed for her son's apartment and tried to think of all the good things she could report about her home repairs.

Aside from meeting a handsome, caring man who'd comforted her during the aftershock and remembering how wonderful it was to be held, if only for a little while, she couldn't think of one good thing to tell Ian.

Oh, well. She sighed. She'd think of something....

CANE CLOSED THE refrigerator door on the marinating flank steak. It would stay there until tomorrow, when he'd cook it until it was tender and ready for the best-tasting fajitas he could produce.

It was ten-thirty at night, and he'd just closed down his computer for the day. His friends were in bed and the apartment was quiet—just the way he liked it. He popped the top off a longneck beer, strolled to the couch and picked up the TV remote. In minutes he was engrossed in a situation comedy, where the girl resembled a freer, easier-going Bernadette. The woman who looked like Bernadette was sure doing strange things to his libido.

Cane tried to ignore that feeling. Leaning his head back, he closed his eyes and went over the list of things he had to do tomorrow. His business was either feast or famine. If there wasn't a catastrophe, he didn't work and was bored every day waiting for something to happen so he could save more money toward his dream—a ranch in Texas hill country that would give him the sense of peace he'd always sought and never found.

But when there was a catastrophe anywhere in the USA, he worked fourteen to eighteen hours a day and it still wasn't enough time to get done what was necessary. Every day was catch-up time and every evening was spent planning for the next day. It was a hectic schedule, but Cane loved it.

Except occasionally, when a moment of quiet made him aware just how alone he was. Oh, he didn't want a woman in his life; they became too complicated and usually wanted—even demanded—much more than he was willing to give. He'd never met one that he was willing to give up his freedom for. He'd certainly never met one for whom he'd ever put his emotions on the line.

But the price of being in control and free enough to call all the shots in his own life and business was to be alone and occasionally lonely. That was the way things were.

Life was tough.

Usually he didn't even think about being by himself. But tonight, with Bernadette Conrad on his mind, he was forced to wonder what it would be like to be emotionally connected to a woman. She was a classy lady who evoked thoughts of home and family and Sunday dinners with children. He certainly wouldn't mind having a fling with her. But was the price too much?

"Yes." The answer came quietly but firmly. He was a normal, healthy male who was spending a little free time daydreaming about a woman who appealed to him. That was all there was to it, and there was no sense making more out of those feelings than there was.

His eyes still closed, he fumbled for the remote control, touched the top button and heard the TV click off. Then, with a sigh, he eased back into the couch and told himself to go to sleep. It didn't matter that he hadn't pulled out the sofa bed; he could sleep just as easily this way as he could the conventional way. And there was no female around to tell him to go to bed.

Somehow, that thought didn't please him as much as it used to....

Cane jumped, startled awake from the dream. She'd been curled in his arms, her head resting on his chest until he tilted her chin up and kissed her firmly on the mouth. Her taste was sweet, her lips soft and vulnerable to his touch, curving slightly to fit his own. Then she let him know he was acceptable to her by kissing him back instead of remaining passive. Her soft hands encircled his neck and a sigh passed between them, making his heart skip several beats. Her body seemed to flow against him, its gentle curves fitting all his hard planes just right. Hands as light as a hummingbird's wings touched him all over. He felt his own need building, and every small, sensual move she made confirmed that she felt just like he did. He'd never felt so lucky, so happy. So complete. Just as he was about to lay her across the bed, she spoke the two words that had the power to wake him up.

"Love me," she whispered.

Heart pounding, groin aching, Cane opened his eyes and stared at the curtained patio doors and wondered where the hell such a stupid dream had come from. Then he remembered the TV program and his thoughts about Bernadette as he'd drifted off to sleep last night. He'd probably programmed himself to dream of her, and more specifically, to dream of making love to a her.

That was it. A single, stupid thought triggered this whole episode. It didn't matter that he hadn't had a dream like that in years. It was just a fluke.

Purposefully, Cane closed his eyes and pretended that he hadn't been awakened by the erotic dream. It didn't work.

Instead, Bernadette's soft, low voice echoed in his mind, hinting of things best not thought about. Her figure, naked and beautiful, danced in front of his eyes.

He had to stop it.

She was a woman who needed commitment. If nothing else told him, his dream emphasized that part of her nature. His gut had told him so earlier, and just now his subconscious had confirmed it.

Besides, it wasn't good to get involved with an insured. Business and pleasure never mixed....

But in the morning while Cane set up to do estimates on the computer, he found himself hoping Bernadette would call. When she finally did in the late afternoon, he was irritated that she'd waited all day.

"I expected you to call me this morning," he stated curtly, his slow drawl all but disappearing in agitation. "Have you found an apartment yet?"

"I've called several complexes, Mr. Mitchell," she replied, her voice sounding just as tired this afternoon as it did yesterday. He had a feeling it wasn't like her at all. "Everything is filled. It seems quite a few people have been displaced by the quake."

Cane muttered a curse under his breath. He should have remembered how hard it was to find a place. Hadn't he and Reed gone through the same thing to find a corporate apartment with all the amenities, like pots, pans, sheets and towels? They'd had to go to the outskirts of this sprawling city to find something they could afford and still make a profit.

"You'll have to look farther out from Los Angeles. Would you like me to try the apartment complex I'm in? I think they might have something available."

"Are they earthquake-proof?"

"Ms. Conrad, it's on rollers and springs built to the newest codes, but nothing is completely earthquake-proof." He almost heard her thoughts, and tried to answer them. "But I'll check at this complex and see what they have available."

"That's wonderful. I'll be doing temporary office work for a while, so it doesn't matter where I live. The way my luck is running lately, any job I get will be across town from wherever I choose." There was a hint of laughter in her voice, but he knew she felt exactly as she'd said: The world wasn't giving her a fair shake and she had no alternative but to ride it out.

"I'll call you back in an hour. Your son's place?"

"No. I rented a hotel room, Mr. Mitchell. I don't think I could have stood another night of listening to Ian whisper to his girlfriend on the phone. It's an invasion of both our privacies."

Cane laughed. Even in the face of adversity, the woman had a sense of humor. He had a feeling that until the quake upset her world, she'd been a very together person. He liked that.

"By the way, Mr. Mitchell, you have a wonderful laugh." Her warm, soft voice complimented him. "You ought to practice it more often."

His smile stayed on his lips. It pleased him to know that he pleased her. "Why, thank you, Ms. Conrad. I appreciate your kind words."

"Those are just the facts. If it was a compliment, I'd throw in more adjectives. I might even get a little flowery. But a comment is usually short, terse and straight to the point, don't you think?"

He laughed again. "Well, I thank you just the same."

"Thank you, Mr. Mitchell. Anytime." Then she hung up with a quiet click.

He was still smiling as he set the cell phone back on his desk. When she wasn't stressed out, she allowed that sexy little streak of humor to show. Interesting. For just a few minutes he indulged himself in wondering what it would be like to have a brief fling with the sexy Ms. Conrad. She was different from any woman he'd met before and that alone intrigued him. She had as much brains as she had class—and she had loads of class.

And she was all wrong for him.

No, that wasn't the case. He was a loner; an aging, angry loner who had gotten this far in life because he was responsible for no one but himself. The fact was he wasn't right for anyone. His marriage had proved that. Especially not a vulnerable widow who was tough enough to make it on her own, but not tough enough to weather a few solid aftershocks.

Cane decided to take a break by going over to the complex office and giving them Bernadette's number. That way he did his job and didn't have to have any contact with her.

Back to work, he told himself. It wasn't easy, but years of training helped him focus on his work with only fleeting thoughts of the soft, enticing appeal of women—and one woman in particular.

BERNADETTE STUCK HER head in the walk-in closet while Margo Reynolds, the assistant manager, a young woman who was as cute as she was bubbly, gave a run-down on the entire complex.

"And the pool and spa are available until eleven at night or probably longer if you're quiet and don't disturb the neighbors."

"Great," Bernadette murmured, glancing at the patio off one of the two large bedrooms. The foothills of the San Gabriel Mountains were etched brownish blue against the pale blue sky. The breeze blew gently, stirring a neighbor's plant leaves and brushing against her cheek.

She felt . . . *itchy*. That was the word that came to mind. Itchy and nervous and slightly tense with waiting. But waiting for what? she asked herself, knowing the answer but not wanting to admit it. The assistant manager had said that Cane Mitchell might join them here so he could okay the apartment cost. Bernadette knew Cane Mitchell didn't have to give his seal of approval, and that all she needed was a signed lease and the insurance company he represented would reimburse her for her expenses. But she wanted to see him again anyway.

"And the washer and dryer connections are in the hallway," the young woman went on.

"Very nice," Bernadette said for lack of anything else to say. It was a beautiful apartment and she loved both it and the view of the mountains. But the apartment wasn't the reason for her sky-high feelings of anticipation.

She wanted to see Cane's brown eyes sparkle, hear that melodious, Texas drawl, feel his arms around her as he tried to comfort—

"So. What do you think?" Margo asked, her perky voice halting the flow of fantasy. "I hate to rush you into a decision, but I'm afraid I have no choice. When Cane called, we promised we'd hold this for twenty-four hours so you could inspect, but . . ." Margo's flawless young face frowned. "I've got several people who are interested if you aren't."

"What's Ms. Conrad not going to like, Margo?"

Both women turned at the male voice. Bernadette felt her smile widen and warm as she watched Cane saunter through the open door toward them. "You've got the corner on mighty fine-looking apartments. And they're big enough to raise a heifer."

"Have you seen that many?" Bernadette asked. A part of her didn't want to know. It meant that he'd been into those apartments and that probably they were rented by women. . . .

"No, ma'am. I didn't have to. Margo, here, told me about all the other apartment complexes and how bad they were." His dimpled grin made Bernadette blush and Margo giggle.

"It's true. None of them can hold a candle to ours." Margo's tone of voice told Bernadette that the assistant manager was probably just as smitten with Cane as she was.

"Why, what a pretty view." Cane stuck his head out the patio door. "It's pretty enough to sit and watch a sunset while drinking one of those margaritas."

"You don't drink margaritas?" Bernadette asked.

"No, ma'am. Beer is my drink of choice."

"Of course," she stated dryly. "It's so . . . Texas."

His knowing grin highlighted deep dimples she would have loved to stroke with a finger. "Yes, ma'am."

Bernadette felt herself turn pink under his intense dark-eyed gaze. She clutched her purse strap and began an inspection of the kitchen. "Nice size."

Margo waxed on about the apartment and Bernadette only half listened. All her concentration was focused on the man who strolled beside her, looking as if he were eating up all of the assistant manager's words.

But Bernadette knew better. When she opened the pantry, he stood so close behind her she could feel his warm breath on her neck. "Plenty of space," he commented softly. "Do you like the place?"

She couldn't move. She didn't want to. If she took just one step back, she would be flat against his body, touching him from neck to knee. "Yes."

"Then snap it up," he whispered.

"Yes."

He turned toward Margo who was standing in the doorway. "Sold, Margo. You got yourself a new tenant." He turned to Bernadette. "Moving in tomorrow?"

"In three days," she corrected. "I can't get a mover any sooner."

"You're storing a bunch of your stuff, aren't you?"

She felt the beginnings of panic. Nothing was done. No boxes packed, no decisions made on what should be stored and what came to her new apartment. "I'm not sure, yet."

"Well, Ms. Conrad," Cane said, reaching for her hand. "Don't panic now, but I saw your house and there's too much stuff for you to bring it all here." He must have seen her anxiety, because his hand tightened, giving hers a light squeeze. "We'll put a steel container in front of your house and you can store your belongings in there. That way you can have access whenever you want it."

She'd seen those containers in front of other people's houses, but had thought they were filled with construction equipment, not personal possessions. "Really? Can't someone steal it?"

"Only if they have the specific truck to move it. No other vehicle will do. I guarantee, even in the worst section of Los Angeles, your goods would be safe in one of those things."

She wanted confirmation. She wanted him to continue holding her hand. "And accessible?"

"And accessible."

"Okay," she said, a smile that refused to be quelled dancing on her mouth.

"What are you doing for dinner?" he asked, still quiet.

"Grabbing a fast-food hamburger. Nothing. Why do you ask?" She hoped he'd say the magic words....

"Can I take you out to some cheap dive to celebrate your new place of living in a style you don't want to become accustomed to?"

The magic words she'd wanted to hear. "I'd love it."

"Good." He turned to the assistant manager standing in the doorway, who watched them with avid interest. "Margo, I'd appreciate it if you'd hold all the paperwork for tomorrow."

"Well." She frowned. "We're not supposed to hold anything without a written lease or agreement..."

Reaching into his pocket, he pulled out a neatly stacked wad of bills. Flipping through them, he withdrew one. "I'll give you a hundred dollars, and if Ms.

Conrad isn't here tomorrow to sign those papers, then you can keep the money. Deal?"

Margo smiled. "Deal."

"Good. Now that the apartment problem is out of the way, Ms. Conrad, how about celebrating with a cheap and tawdry dinner someplace where the light is worse than the food and the food is barely edible? That way we can lose weight and enjoy ourselves at the same time. All on an adjuster's salary, of course."

Bernadette couldn't help the laughter that bubbled out. Just being with him made her smile. His humor had to affect her even more so. "I heard adjusters were paid handsomely."

"Vicious rumors. That's all they are." He shook his head as if in mock tragedy. "Vicious rumors put out by insurance agents who wished they could travel the world without paying their dues by getting a tattoo and joining the navy—or by becoming a catastrophe adjuster."

She was amazed at her own continuous laughter. She hadn't laughed this much in a very long time. "Poor you," she crooned.

"It's about time you caught on to me, woman. I need all the sympathy you can stand to give. After all, I'm all alone in the world—next thing to an orphan—and have nobody to help me through life. I'm in a job whose stress level is so high, cows can't jump over it. And now I'm taking a beautiful woman to eat in a restaurant that hasn't got enough light for me to gaze longingly into her eyes and whisper sweet nothings—even if I was smart enough to know nothing to whisper into her ear."

"Such problems," she murmured, allowing herself to be led out the door and into the apartment hallway, where Margo had discreetly waited for them.

After locking the apartment, they walked to the elevator. Then, with a wave goodbye to Margo, Cane led Bernadette to the underground parking garage and his truck, giving her a quick tour of the pool, spa and trash bins on the way. "I gather we're going in your car," she said dryly.

"Truck," he corrected before shutting the door and walking around the front of the vehicle.

They drove down Brand Boulevard in the big black GMC truck with the extended cab area that made up into a back seat. The radio with special speakers bellowed out a low and moaning country song by some guy who was all stopped up or had a cold, she was sure. It was the saddest song she'd ever heard, but it still didn't wipe the smile off her face or replace the giddy happiness in her heart.

They ate outdoors at an Italian restaurant. Their table was surrounded by lush plants and covered with an umbrella. Bernadette hadn't even known such restaurants existed in this new neck of the woods, but she enjoyed the people-watching as much as she enjoyed the company. Once the waiter took their order and delivered wine and a bottle of beer for Cane, she sat back and relaxed. The wine was delicious, helping her relax even more.

Cane sat across from her, his long legs straight out to the side and crossed. He looked like the most relaxed man in the world.

"Did your parents call you Bernadette, or did they come up with a neat nickname and only call you that when they were angry?" Cane asked.

"How perceptive. My parents called me by my middle name, which is Marie. It wasn't until I married straight out of high school that I called myself Bernadette. That was because my husband always called me that. He loved it, even though he hated all the nicknames: Bee, Bernie, Detta. Now I'm so used to it, I don't think I'd answer to anything else."

"No one ever called you Bette?"

"No one."

When the food was brought, Bernadette decided to turn the tables. "How about you? Did your parents call you Cane because they needed to take one to you on occasion?"

"My daddy named me 'Hurricane' because I was born in the middle of one." His voice was light, but the narrowness of his gaze told her he didn't want to discuss it.

But she wanted to know. "And your mother went along with it?"

"My mother had no choice. She did as she was told."

Her brows rose. "Really. How sad."

"Yes, it was." He expertly twirled his spaghetti on his fork. "But I wasn't responsible for their sadness. I just added to it."

She could feel the pain of everything he wasn't saying. But she also knew she couldn't let her sympathy show. Her instincts told her that Cane wouldn't handle that emotion as well as he could the initial rejection. "That must have been tough."

Cane shrugged, but didn't look at her. "Maybe, but I didn't know any better, so it was normal to me."

It was time to move on to a safer subject. She had the feeling she wouldn't hear the rest of the story until they knew each other better—much better. That might mean never. "Do you have any children, Mr. Mitchell?"

"No, I never had the good fortune. But I like to think I will someday."

She felt a stab of jealousy. "Really? Have you got the mother of your future children all picked out?"

"No, ma'am. Not yet. Whoever she is, she hasn't decided to enter my life yet, which proves she's got more brains than I do. She'd have to be a fool or a saint to stick with me and still have other children under her wing."

"Meaning you're child enough to mother?"

He grinned widely. "I knew you'd understand."

It was a warning, she was sure. And one that she would heed, no matter how drawn to the man she was. "Only too well, Mr. Mitchell. Only too well."

At the end of the meal, he escorted her to the truck to drive her back to her car. During their meal, the sun had set spectacularly, and now darkness enveloped them, making the interior of the cab far more intimate than Bernadette felt comfortable with. Cane's expression showed that he felt the same way."

"Do you have a moving company you'd like to use?" he asked politely.

"No, and I haven't packed or—"

"The movers can do that," he stated, knowing what she was going to say. "Call around in the morning. Some of the big ones can pack you the next day, then move what furniture you want into the apartment the day after that."

"How long do you think it will take to fix my house?" she asked, suddenly returning to the reality of being homeless—even for a little while.

Cane thought for a moment. "From what damage I saw, a couple of months should do it. But the contractor could change that opinion as soon as he tears into the walls." He grinned. "However, the first thing on the list is to get your belongings out. Then your contractor can begin work." His warm brown eyes stared into hers. "Everything starts with a first step, Bernadette," he said, using her given name for the first time. "Don't feel overwhelmed. Let's just take one step at a time. It will all work out."

"Yes, but I need it to work out in my favor—not just *work*."

His grin was liquid and more charming than any she'd ever seen. "You want it all, don't you?" he teased.

She felt herself relax a little. "But of course. Don't we all?"

"I never thought of it that way, Ms. Conrad, but I reckon so. In that case, I'll change my mind. Don't worry, this will all work out in your favor, ma'am. It's my job to see that both you and the insurance company come out winners." He stood just an inch closer, taking away her breath with the motion. "And I thank you for making this ole country boy happy by sharing a meal."

"You're just full of it, aren't you?"

"Of what?"

"Charm and blarney," she answered.

He hesitated before a twinkle lit his gaze. "Yes, ma'am. I am."

She tried not to smile, but it didn't work. "Thank you for a straight answer." She held out her hand. "And a wonderful dinner."

Cane took her hand in his and shook it, his palm warm and callused. "You're quite welcome. I'll be in all day tomorrow. Give me a call and let me know your progress."

As Bernadette drove away, she saw Cane Mitchell in her rearview mirror. She was amazed at her reaction. She didn't like seeing him disappearing from her sight.

She didn't like it one bit. . . .

# 3

THE NEXT FEW DAYS were so busy, Bernadette barely had
time to breathe. Instead of making her feel harried, or-
ganizing the move gave her a sense of accomplish-
ment—as if she were back in control of her life. She felt
competent again. She'd needed that. Since the earthquake she'd been emotionally off-kilter, but the activ-
ity of the past few days had given her back her much-
needed "sea legs" for dealing with life's unexpected
problems.

Ian helped by boxing up his own roomful of belongings and sorting through the garage for her, but there
was still so much to be done. During that time, she'd
also managed to run back to Glendale to sign a lease
agreement, make plans for the utilities to be turned on
and get a new phone number while retaining the old
one. And all the time, thoughts of the sexy and competent Hurricane Mitchell were never far from her
mind.

He was never far from her ear, either. Every time she
took action on another seemingly insurmountable
problem, it was because of his good advice. They spoke
on the phone at least twice a day, Bernadette telling him
about her newest difficulty and Cane giving her a no-
nonsense solution or alternative. He had answers to her

thousands of questions about moving, contractors and rentals, and he gave them readily and with humor. He eased not only her mind but her tension, too. She'd never had a male combination mentor and friend before, and found it both comforting and scary. Since Nick's death, she'd never relied on anyone, and had thought she never would again.

But lately, just the sound of Cane's drawl on the phone made her heart pump faster and her nipples harden—even when he was speaking about such everyday matters as contractors, movers and storage containers. She was glad he couldn't see her reaction to his voice. Only heaven knew how she would have acted if he'd been standing in front of her!

Although she realized how wonderful having his arms around her had been, she hadn't known till that moment just how much she missed the sound of a male voice, the scent of a man, the touch of a male hand. Her response had been so immediate and so strong, she needed to stand away from the situation for a little while to get a better handle on her feelings.

She finally told herself that it was simply a male touch she'd missed. A male voice. She refused to believe it could be this particular male.

Bernadette didn't need any man in her life.

But Cane was different. Besides, she'd learned that she could talk to him about anything and he was both knowledgeable and helpful. However, when the conversation became the least bit personal on his end, he backed away. This was a man who was not into any kind of commitment. Either that, or he was already emotionally committed elsewhere.

That thought acted like a prick to a balloon. Whatever the reason, Mr. Cane Mitchell was as prickly as a porcupine when it came to man-woman emotional stuff—at least, with her....

Moving day came. Ian, trying to emphasize how grown-up and manly he was, helped with the packing one day and sorting the next. Everything had to be watched and gone through, because as the house was emptied belongings went into either the moving truck or the large steel container.

That done, Bernadette locked the door on her empty house and led the way to her new apartment. She tried not to look back and realize the hollow shell she was leaving was her home of so many years. Instead, she told herself it was just another impersonal piece of property that was going to be renovated.

The moving men followed her to Glendale and unloaded the few pieces of furniture she'd chosen to take with her to the new apartment instead of storing in the steel container now sitting in front of her house. They even helped unpack the kitchen items—not that she'd brought many of them.

The apartment wasn't as big as her home, but it was certainly bigger than she needed for a three-month stay. Ever since her son had moved into his first apartment last month, she'd been feeling the emptiness of her house. It was no different here. After years of taking care of someone, she now had no one but herself to watch out for on a daily basis.

The only apartments the complex had available was the tiniest one-bedroom she'd ever seen, and this two-bedroom with a den. Since her choice was limited, she'd taken the bigger of the two apartments in the hopes that her son would join her. She'd known better, but she asked anyway.

Ian's expression was crestfallen. "Ah, jeez, Mom," he groaned. "We just got the place fixed up the way we like it. We've got eight speakers for our stereo now, and can hear the music everywhere. I planned all the electronics for it, and I don't want to give that up." He placed his hands on his hips and looked around the house he was raised in. "I don't think the apartment you're moving to would let me play hard rock above a whisper any more than you would let me do it here."

He reminded her how often she'd had to tell him to turn down the sound. She had to try a different tact. "Yes, but you could live here rent-free for a while. That would help, wouldn't it? You wouldn't have to work so hard at waitering for your extra money."

It didn't seem to help. "But, Mom, I'd lose my place at the house. Besides, you wouldn't want me to lose this opportunity to grow and become self-sufficient, would you?" He grinned endearingly, placing an arm around his mother. "I'm not a baby anymore. You said I had to grow up. This is part of it, isn't it?"

Bernadette knew when she was licked. And he was right. She was asking too much of Ian, who was just experiencing his first taste of freedom and loving it. Why would he give that up just to please a mom and postpone her symptoms of empty nest syndrome?

Some habits were hard to break. For so long it had been just the two of them against the world that she sometimes forgot not to treat him like a child.

Instead, she hid the sadness she felt. She smiled. "That's fine, honey. It was just a suggestion."

His relieved smile was her reward.

Ian and his roommate, Hans, were a great help in both the packing and unpacking stages, and things went much more smoothly than even she had imagined. It had taken two days, but she was now moved in and things were in relatively good order.

Now that she was alone, she craved another human face to look at—a human conversation to indulge in, even if it was only about the weather. This feeling of loneliness was something new to her. Other than missing her husband, Bernadette had never felt the need for human contact; she'd been thrilled with the quiet and the opportunity to work at home.

When the moving crew left, Bernadette straightened up a knickknack here and there, and put away an item or two. It didn't take long, the crew had unpacked everything and she'd had the supervising help of her son. But Ian had placed a kiss on her cheek and raced out the door shortly after the crew, saying something about a party with the guys.

Although it had been a very long day, Bernadette's nerves were stretched taut. She felt antsy—again. She slipped on a pair of sneakers and hooked her new set of keys to her shorts, then headed out the door. Perhaps a walk would give her a different perspective.

Heading out the gate to the sidewalk, she picked up the pace, walking quickly down the tree-lined street toward . . . she didn't know where. Ten minutes later a sign pointed the way to a historic house and grounds, and she decided to follow it. The uphill climb felt good to her.

When she walked through the gates of the historic park, she realized it was an original settler's home and grounds. To the left of the gate was a long rectangular house, stuccoed and with a wide, shaded veranda. To the right were the gardens. In one corner was a couple standing in front of a minister, reciting vows while a smattering of friends and family watched on.

Bernadette sat on the concrete bench under a wide-spreading umbrella tree and watched. The ceremony brought back all the memories of her own wedding. It had been an elopement—hurried, exciting and frightening. They'd driven to Mexico with some friends. From the very beginning, it had all the earmarks of a failing marriage: they were both in their teens, their parents disapproved—and she was two months pregnant.

Despite the initial problems, the marriage had worked. Two months later, she'd lost that child. They had cried for the dreams that died with the little one, but had gone on, confident that life lay in front of them, and ready to show the rest of the world.

Maybe because there was no one to help them, she and Nick had depended upon each other, bonded together, and their love had grown stronger. Ian had added to their contentment.

The newly wedded couple kissed and the few guests clapped and ahhed. Tears filled Bernadette's eyes, but they weren't tears of pain and loss. They were tears of joy for the two she just had witnessed marrying. She hoped they found the happiness she had found. She hoped they continued to work at loving each other.

Even knowing that she would end up a struggling widow, she would take that path with Nick again. She had twelve years of wonderful memories. If she had any regret at all, it was just that she should have said "I love you" far more often than she had.

With a sigh, Bernadette stood and began her trek back toward the apartment, taking a slightly different route. It was dusk and the usual evening traffic had picked up its pace.

She rounded a corner and spotted a frozen-yogurt parlor. Scores of kids sat around concrete tables and benches licking waffle cones piled high with wild and obviously tasty colors.

And sitting on a side bench was Cane, jeans-clad legs stretched out in front of him, crossed at the ankles. A clingy knit shirt accentuated his better-than-nice build and taut stomach. Dark glasses were perched on top of his breeze-blown blond-streaked hair. She watched him swipe his tongue around the side of his chocolate cone. Her heart skipped a beat.

She leaned against an unlit streetlamp and waited for the light to change—waited for him to focus his attention somewhere else. Waited . . .

She followed his riveted gaze. It was focused on a teenager who looked like she was baby-sitting, and a chubby baby boy sitting ramrod straight in a stroller. His little face was covered in chocolate ice cream, his grin as big as his round face. He held a small cone in both hands on his lap and was trying to tackle it directly by plunging his mouth right down inside of it.

Bernadette couldn't help but smile, but when she looked back at Cane, her smile slowly drooped until it slid away. His gaze held such a deep yearning, it hurt her heart to see such a look on his face.

His gaze drifted away from the child and he spotted her. It took a minute for him to bury his hungry expression and for his twinkling dark eyes and carefree smile to come into play. The public facade, she thought. The Cane everyone knew—and no one knew.

It wasn't that different from the Bernadette everyone thought they knew, too. Both were defenses—something to keep the world at bay.

He stood as she approached. "Hi, neighbor. I see you've found my weakness," he said, holding up his unfinished cone. "Can I buy you one?"

"I'd love it," she stated with a smile, knowing she wasn't going to taste a bite of it. "Chocolate-with-nuts yogurt."

"You've got it. Stay right here." He pointed to the pink-umbrellaed round table and benches. "Seats are at a premium at this time of day." A moment later, Cane disappeared into the store and stood in line with several others, waiting for his chance to order.

Bernadette sat on the concrete bench and watched the others around her, but her real attention was focused on the handsome blond-haired man who finally walked out carrying her ice-cream cone.

"Thank you," she said, reaching for the cone he held out to her. "I'm not sure, but isn't this considered above and beyond the call of duty as an insurance adjuster?"

"Not at all," he claimed, sitting beside her and leaning back negligently. "We do whatever we can to make our insureds comfortable. It's in the adjuster code—or at least it should be. As long as it's all within the limits of decorum, of course," he added, tongue in cheek.

"Of course." She licked at the side of the cone where a drip was beginning. Its icy chocolate taste was refreshing.

"How's the apartment working out?" His voice sounded tight, and she wondered why. "Are you all moved in and settled?"

She gave him a searching look, but found nothing out of the ordinary. "Wonderful. I've unpacked and think I even know where everything is. What I don't know is how the work on the house will progress. The contractor I called says it will be another two weeks before he can even begin to tear up carpet."

Cane leaned back and stared out at the crowd again, but this time he didn't look pointedly at the little children. "Contractors have got so much work from the earthquake, they can afford to be choosy. At least you have one who knows his stuff."

"Think so?"

"Definitely." Cane's voice was low and sexy. She could have listened all evening and it wouldn't have been enough. "He impressed me because he knew every new code upgrade and how it affected the housing industry."

"You spoke to him?"

Cane nodded. "The minute you hired him, he called to let me know he was on the job."

"Now I'm impressed." And relieved, she wanted to add. She trusted Cane's judgment and his way of doing business.

But Cane was ready to change the subject. "Now, tell me. Is your son moving in with you? You mentioned that you hoped he might."

Bernadette remembered the discussion she'd had with Ian. "No, he's happy where he is. But at least he has the option. Goodness knows, I've got enough room."

"You don't have to sound so down about it. I should think that would make you happy."

She wouldn't admit to how odd it felt to be alone after all these years. It would have been nice to get adjusted to one thing at a time, instead of all at once. But it wasn't to be. So, she smiled. "It does. It also makes me realize just how alone I am."

"Does 'alone' also mean lonely?"

Bernadette was startled by Cane's candor. She hadn't expected it, but she liked it. "Alone just means alone. I was always so busy trying to earn a living, I never had time to realize I was alone before."

"You weren't. You had a son."

She nodded. "But a little boy isn't the same thing as an adult. In those early days of widowhood, I had no one to make decisions, to share burdens, to help carry happiness."

"Happiness?" Cane made it sound like an incomprehensible foreign word.

"You know. The stuff that smiles are made of."

"Oh, I've heard of it." He grinned. "But I've never had enough to carry, let alone needing help to carry it."

She wondered if he knew how sad that sounded. "You sound disillusioned."

"Not at all. I'm a realist." He implied how far smiles were from reality. "Happiness is a lot to ask of life. Even the Constitution says that you're only granted the right to *pursue* it." She could see him building that wall around his emotions as quickly as he had the other times.

"The Constitution was written to serve the common man. Anyone can reach a state of happiness without too much trouble on their part. All they have to do is separate the things they enjoy from the things they don't, and focus on them."

"Yes, Mrs. Pollyanna," he replied in a singsong voice that made her laugh.

"I'm serious, and you're full of—"

"Fun?" he interjected, a twinkle in his eyes. "The devil? Nonsense? Or could it be . . . truth?"

"Maybe it is truth, but I won't apologize for my viewpoint, either. It's also truth. I worked long and hard to be optimistic. And starting tomorrow, I have to be even more so, so don't pop my bubble with your brand of reality yet."

"Why tomorrow?"

"I have to beat the bushes for clients all over again. I need work, Mr. Mitchell. I need work now."

He took another swipe at his cone. "Can you do an estimating program?"

Her brows rose and she stared at him for a moment, ignoring her cone. She hoped . . . "Can you?"

"Yes."

"Then I can do the same thing if you give me an hour of tutoring."

Cane frowned as he stared at her. "Are you sure?"

Bernadette grinned. "I know nineteen different computer programs in my sleep, from landscaping to word processing and accounting to database. One estimating program should be a snap to learn."

He looked down at his empty cone and continued to frown, puzzling something out in his mind. "And you have all the other equipment, don't you?"

"One direct-line fax, a computer, a laser printer, a copier, a calculator, et cetera. You name it and I've got it. I even have the equipment to put together desktop-published spiral notebooks."

He looked surprised and impressed. She liked that about him. When Cane wanted it, he had a very expressive face.

"Do you know anything about insurance adjusting?"

"I have an idea. After all, I'm part of the system now. Remember?"

He was forced to grin. "It's just a vague memory. We just closed your file so we could pay you, didn't we?"

"Yes. But you told me I could open it if any other damage was found."

"That's right." Cane stared up at the darkening sky, and the silence drifted comfortably between them. More teenagers came up and ordered cones, more families drifted by with babies in tow as they leisurely walked back to their homes. Bernadette envied them all. She had wanted a dozen children, not just one. And she had wanted to grow old with her husband, not bury him at an age when they should be looking forward to the future. She had wanted someone to love her enough to stroll down the street and buy her an ice-cream cone.

It hadn't seemed like that much to ask. . . .

"Bernadette, how much would you charge for working on my files?"

Her heart skipped a beat at the thought. She purposely settled a distant inquisitive look on her face. "What does it entail?"

"Keeping an investigation log—an itinerary of everything that's been done on each individual case file. It's fairly simple, just time-consuming."

"How many files?"

"Oh, about a hundred and twenty."

Her heart beat even faster. It was the answer to her prayers. She gave him a price per hour that she thought would seem fair to him.

"Sounds reasonable," he finally said in that husky voice that touched her.

Bernadette let out her breath. "Why don't we try it and see what happens?"

"Tomorrow?" Then he snapped his fingers as memory served him. "No, not tomorrow. I have to scope out a loss site. The next day."

"Where is your loss site?"

"In canyon country, north of here."

"Why don't I go with you? That way I can see what you have to do in your work and know the procedure you're talking about. It will work out best for both of us."

"It's not that interesting."

"It will be for an outsider," she persisted. Bernadette ignored his reluctance to have her with him. Aside from wanting to see what he did for a living in a more up-close and personal way, she needed to be active and busy again. This was an opportunity to do so. "Besides, I'd like to see what you do with other claims. It will give me more insight into the job—assuming you want to trust me with your files."

His grin was as endearing as it was sexy. "I'm not crazy. I'd love for someone to help me. I spend too much time on paperwork as it is."

He stood and stretched, and Bernadette, usually calm and collected around men, had to swallow hard and look away. Her cone dripped onto her fingers, reminding her to eat her sweet. She did so, swiping her tongue around the icy trail. At least it took her attention away from the man in front of her.

"That means you'll have to be ready to go by eight in the morning. First appointment is at nine-thirty."

"That's easy," she assured him. "I used to leave the house at seven when I was a legal secretary."

"It's gonna be a long day." There was his warning again. She wondered what he was warning her about. The job? Being with him all that time?

She didn't see a downside to either alternative. "I'll be ready," she promised. "And I'll be sure to get a good night's rest so you can't accuse me of sleeping on the job."

A strange look crossed his face, then disappeared. "That doesn't sound like your kind of behavior," he said, his tone distant. He dropped his cone in the nearest receptacle and turned in the direction of the apartment. "I'll see you in the morning, then."

"I'll be ready," she promised. "Have a great evening."

Cane didn't answer. Instead, he gave a wave over his shoulder and sauntered down the street that led to his home—and hers. Too bad they were at the same place, she thought, then discarded the intimate image as quickly as it came.

What was the matter with her lately? Cane Mitchell was just another man in a sea of men. He wasn't a god, or a superhero that she should worship. He wasn't a social animal, either, judging from the way he behaved.

Then why was she drawn to him? *What a silly question*, she chided herself. He was good-looking, warm and sexy.

She stood and tossed the rest of the dripping cone in the same receptacle that Cane had used. After wiping her hands on a napkin, she began the walk back to her apartment. Cane had already disappeared around the corner. She wished he'd waited for her—just for the conversation, of course.

That evening she cooked a solitary meal for herself in her new surroundings and cleaned up the kitchen afterward. It was an odd feeling to be here instead of in the house where she'd lived, the kitchen where she'd cooked for herself and her son for the past twelve years. A few years ago she had even imagined herself growing old there ... dying there. That was before the earthquake, when her whole world was turned upside down.

Now, here she was, looking out at an unfamiliar courtyard through a strange window in her new kitchen.

And tomorrow she would begin a new job with a man who was handsome and sexy.

As she crawled into bed, her weary body told her to be happy.

Besides, tomorrow was an interesting day to look forward to. *Get real,* she thought. Probably any day with Cane Mitchell would be interesting.

BERNADETTE COULDN'T HELP but smile when she opened the door the next morning and saw Cane standing there with a grin on his face.

He wore the uniform she was familiar with: black slacks and a white shirt with an insurance insignia on one pocket. A pair of expensive ostrich-skin boots completed the look. His sandy-blond hair was darker because it was still wet from his shower. A light-scented after-shave wafted through the portal and she took an enjoyable deep breath.

"You're early." She opened the door wider. "Give me a minute and I'll get my stuff."

Cane sniffed the air. "Is that coffee?"

"Yes," she called over her shoulder. "Help yourself. Cups are above the pot, and cream is in the fridge."

She reached for her purse and took one last glance in the mirror. Her dark hair was parted on one side and brushed into a soft pageboy with a slight puff of bangs. Because she knew he wore dark jeans, she'd dressed casual, too: khaki pants, a white T-shirt and brown loafers. She looked good and she was thankful. "Nervous" seemed to have been her middle name lately, but today, being with Cane, she needed all the self-confidence she could muster.

Cane was leaning against her kitchen counter, sipping from a steaming mug. "You make good coffee," he commented. "Better than most and almost as good as mine."

She raised a brow. "Thank you, I think," she stated dryly, trying to keep her voice light. "Only a true coffee-drinker would know the difference, of course."

"Of course." He looked around appreciatively at all her kitchen gadgets. "You've got a nice setup here. All the comforts of home."

"It is home. At least for now."

"Sorry." He gave her a sheepish grin. "I was thinking more of myself. I love to cook, and your gadgets remind me of mine. Except that all mine are back in Texas." Cane set his cup down in the sink and rinsed it with water.

The simple act brought him very close to her, but she didn't move. She didn't want to. Besides, in just a moment he would move back to his own space and this tingling feeling would go. "I didn't realize. But I guess it is silly to carry it all with you." Bernadette glanced around, seeing the items from his point of view. "Anytime you feel like cooking, please be my guest. Anything you need to borrow, just shout. It's the least I can do."

His eyes lit up like those of a small boy who'd just been given a bunch of money for toys. "Really?"

She smiled, delighted that such a small thing could make him so happy, and that she'd been able to do it for him. "Really. Anytime."

"That's real neighborly of you," he said with a grin. But his voice lowered as he stared down at her parted lips. The smile slowly disappeared.

Bernadette's eyes fastened on his mouth. Her breath came lightly, then it didn't come at all. Her lips moved, but no words filled the air. Instead, she studied him as hard as he studied her.

Then his head blocked her sight, everything. And his lips brushed against hers, stirring so lightly she wasn't sure if it happened—until it happened again. Her mouth parted even more.

Silently allowing him access.

Neither touched. Neither moved. Their lips met and danced away, then met again. Bernadette's heart raced so fast she thought she would faint from the rush. Everything in her cried out for him to complete the kiss, to take her in his arms and finish what he'd started.

And when he did, she groaned in relief. His arms came around her waist to pull her toward his hard chest. His mouth claimed hers, branding her with heat and imprinting her body with his. They touched head to knee, and the feeling was warm and exquisite.

Cane's tongue danced against hers. Heat invaded her every limb. She wrapped her arms around his neck and clung to him, pressing her breasts against his hard chest. She tilted her head and allowed her own tongue to lead the dance, feeling his body stiffen in almost instant response. Her own groan was answered by one from him.

When he pulled away, she felt bereft. His forehead touched hers as they both tried to catch their breath.

Then, suddenly, his hands dropped from her waist and he took a step back. The open, warm expression he'd shown earlier was gone, replaced by one that was closed, guarded and filled with distaste.

"I'm sorry. I didn't mean to do that." His words were clipped, terse, and cut like a knife.

She leaned back as if slapped. "Neither did I. But it's understandable. We're both out of our element right now. I guess it's normal to reach out to another in a time of crisis." She said the words but it sounded as if she was reading from some clinical report. And she didn't mean one damn word of it!

"I'm not in crisis." His voice broke and he turned to the sink. "Damn," he muttered under his breath.

What had she expected? Love? *Get real,* she told herself, even as she felt her skin flush.

"Well, for the last couple of weeks, 'crisis' has been my middle name," she snapped back. Good grief! Did he think she was so desperate that she would latch on to anyone for comfort? "But I know mistakes when I make one. And that was a big one."

"Damn, don't I know it," he said, running an agitated hand through his blond hair. "Bette, I'm sorry. That never should have happened. If I'd known..."

Bernadette stood a little straighter, her chin tilting upward in defiance.

"The name's Bernadette. And now that we've both got that little piece of curiosity out of the way and we know we're not suited, what say we get going?" She smiled brightly in his direction without looking at him.

She was going to make it through this day even if it killed her. "Should I put some more coffee in a thermos or just grab a cup to take on the road? I have a few to-go cups."

Silence greeted her words.

Her heart thudded heavily in her breast as she began looking for the plastic cups she'd seen just yesterday when unpacking.

Finally, Cane cleared his throat. "Bernadette, I—"

But she interrupted him. She didn't want to rehash the embarrassment of hearing his reasons for not wanting her. Some other time. But not now. And she knew that she never, ever, wanted a repeat of this performance. It was too humiliating. "Let's get going, okay? Traffic will be tough enough this morning without me making you late on top of it all."

"Ready?"

Hurricane Mitchell gave a deep sigh and turned toward the door. "Ready," he echoed. But he knew he wasn't.

Instead, he was scared. . . .

# 4

CANE DROVE UP THE MAIN highway into canyon country, telling his senses to ignore Bernadette sitting beside him. *Just focus on the task at hand*, he told himself. Still, his mind buzzed with emotions that had nothing to do with work.

He'd kissed Bernadette and almost lost his senses, whirling into a void that beat Alice in Wonderland's rabbit hole all to hell and gone.

Did she really have no reaction to that kiss? Or had she lied? Her response had seemed to be as strong as his until he'd stepped back and seen the look in her eyes. She had looked scared and shocked. Was he that bad? Was he such a turnoff that his kiss, his touch didn't affect her at all?

More than his feelings were hurt by her indifferent reaction. It was that same old sense of inadequacy, of not being up to par, that surfaced from deep inside him at her lack of response. It brought back all those old, nasty thoughts that ate at him like a vulture pecking away at carrion.

Who the hell did Cane think he was that he could appeal to a woman as classy and savvy as Bernadette Conrad? She hadn't grown up in the back streets of Galveston. She didn't know the degradation of having parents who were whores and addicts. She had no idea how far he'd already come on the road of life.

*Face it*, Mitchell, he told himself. *She doesn't know a damn thing about the kind of home you were born into.*

He'd bet that Bernadette was a sheltered woman who had gone from her loving parents to a husband who loved her. Even in widowhood, she'd been granted a child to raise, upon whom she could lavish more love. Although she probably didn't realize it, Bernadette had never been without a strong emotional connection. She'd likely never known the fear of being completely alone—especially in her youth, when it counted the most. And never worried about not being loved—by anyone. Compared to him, she was a babe in the dark and treacherous forest of life.

He finally gave in to his needs and glanced over at her. She sat stiffly in the seat of his truck, staring straight ahead at the hills. Her small chin was tilted at a slightly determined angle, but her features were soft and feminine. Her dark hair glistened in a shaft of sunlight through the back window and her delicate hands rested in her lap, manicured fingers laced together.

How wonderful for her that she didn't know the sordid kind of life he'd known. That experience would have turned her into a distrusting loner, too.

These thoughts just verified his original impression that it was too late for either of them to change or become anything other than what they already were. Time had done its job and made them who they were today. Better that he kill those silent but errant thoughts of home and love and companionship. They were nothing but dreams. Life had proved that to him at an early age.

"Such beautiful country," she murmured. A soft gray haze of dust filtered around each giant boulderlike hunk of land strutting up from the earth. "Looks like Camelot, doesn't it?" she said.

He followed her glance back out the window at the winding highway and traffic. Stores lined the freeway exits with signs proclaiming the next exit, the next deal, the next whatever. "It would be if there wasn't a house perched on every crag, near every gully. Why do you all build your houses so precariously when you know you're in earthquake country and everything you own, including your own carcass, could wind up at the bottom of the hill?"

"I'm not sure," she mused. "It could be that we're thumbing our nose at Mother Nature. Or maybe it's because of the view." She grinned impishly and he had to stop himself from pulling over and kissing her. "Don't you Texans try to defy nature, too?"

Cane had the grace to look sheepish. "No, ma'am. Except in the West Texas desert or in the hill country north of San Antonio, Texas doesn't have a high spot to call our own. We've got flat prairie land as far as the eye can see. It's so flat in some places that people drive to an overpass just to see a change of scene from above."

Bernadette grinned. "Then I guess you're envious of our beautiful terrain."

"Yes, ma'am."

"And I guess you'd like to have some of it."

"Yes, ma'am."

"And I think you'd enjoy mountain climbing just as much as we do."

"Yes, ma'am. Especially if I could see something when I got to the top."

She became silent for a moment. "When I was young and just married, we used to go hiking all over the state. It was so beautiful. I never saw a view I didn't like."

"And later? Did you continue hiking?"

"No." Her tone turned regretful. "Ian came along and we got caught up in careers, child raising, gardening and all those other everyday things. Our usual family outside activities consisted of picnics at the beach or going to the movies together. But now, I wish we'd kept it up. Ian would have grown to enjoy it. As it is now, he hardly leaves the city unless he's going to Zuma Beach to surf."

Everyday things, she'd said. They'd been everyday and ordinary to her and to her son, but were the very things Cane had craved as a child. He'd never had those close family times that made loving, memorable moments. And she had lost them. He didn't know which was worse, but he'd bet even money that knowing and enjoying everyday daily patterns of life with someone you loved and who loved you, and then losing that person, was worse than never knowing.

He wanted to comfort her, release some of the pain he saw flash across her face. "Everyone's got a bag full of regrets they carry through life, Bernadette. That's what life is filled with. If that's a sample of yours, you oughta be able to heft it in one hand."

Her laughter was low, catching in her throat. "Wouldn't that be nice if it was true? However, I think people carry more guilt than regret. And we all know how heavy guilt can be." She sighed and gave a small smile that branded into his heart. "But what I just commented on was only a passing sadness, not a regret. I know. I already have enough of both to last a lifetime."

"Well, that must be a heavy load."

"And what about you, Cane? What are a few of your regrets?" she asked.

That was a question he didn't want to delve into. "Me? Well, I travel so fast, I don't have time to chase those thoughts. But if I had to pick one, it would be that I never get to see enough of this country. I do my job, then move on too quickly to take the time to enjoy it." He was proud of that throwaway answer. Let her make something of it.

Cane wondered what regrets or sadness she could possibly have endured, but his exit was just ahead, and he had to pay attention to the written directions to get to the first loss site.

However, he was curious about what her sorrows and regrets were. He wanted to know more. He wanted to soothe her sorrows. He wanted to share her joys. For the first time he wanted to get emotionally close to a woman. The woman now seated beside him.

*Face it,* his mind prodded harshly. *The truth is you want to make love to her and you think knowing her sorrows might give you some insight into how to get her into your bed.*

Bernadette looked down at the directions scribbled on the file lying between them. "Turn right, here."

"Thanks, navigator," he said, turning the corner on a yellow light.

Cane forced himself to think of other things besides the woman beside him. This wasn't the time for crazy sexual fantasies. But he promised himself that later he would ask the thousands of questions that popped up from their conversation. Maybe tonight . . .

That thought had his head spinning again.

Bernadette kept her eyes straight ahead or on the file between them. She didn't want to inadvertently react to Cane—and she certainly didn't want him to know if she did!

Her mind kept replaying the scene in the kitchen until it ignited a fire deep inside her, reminding her of the days when she was married, felt romantic and could act out the longings she'd shared with the man she cared about most in the world. But this wasn't one of those times, and she couldn't play out erotic fantasies that popped up and taunted her.

She stole a glance at Cane. His expression was forbidding, almost angry. Was he thinking about this morning? Did he regret kissing her so much that he wished he hadn't brought her along? Well, at least it was too late for that. Perhaps if she was quiet enough, he'd forget that kiss and they could get back on a friendly footing.

She missed the rapport they'd so recently established. She missed his smile, his laughing eyes. And yet she had no right to those things. They weren't hers to begin with.

But her imagination wasn't listening; it kept creating scenarios anyway. About Cane holding her in his arms on the darkened balcony overlooking the valley. Or kissing her, naked, while the sunset poured over them. . . .

A shiver shot up her spine at the erotic images.

Finally Cane pulled the truck to a stop in front of an old, two-story natural-stone home. It was located in one of the few older areas in the surrounding hills of Northridge. Most of the homes were brand-new and in some type of subdivision, but this neighborhood was on the secluded side of a hill. The terrain was filled with boulders and large, thick trees.

"Ready?" Cane reached into the back of the truck and grabbed a small case he attached to his belt. Then he opened his door.

She took the file and clipboard it was attached to, and tucked it under her arm. "Ready."

Bernadette fell in love with the old stone house. Built by a famous comic actor in the late thirties as a getaway home, it had all the charm and personality of its era. And a few wonderful surprises.

Damage was minimal, but the tour through the home was something Bernadette wouldn't forget. Gleaming antiques filled the rooms, wood floors shone, wonderful warm colors accented every nook and cranny. Cane measured and photographed each and every room until they wound up at the back of the house.

There were two rooms here that took her breath away. On the first floor was a large room with a billiard table in the center. The walls and floors shimmered with an unusual wavering blue light. When she looked up, her breath caught in her throat.

"Only in Hollywood," Cane murmured, staring at the ceiling.

"This isn't Hollywood," she corrected. "It's Newhall."

"Same thing."

"What is it?" she asked, but she already knew.

"It's a glass-bottomed pool."

"Only in Hollywood," she repeated.

"Well built."

"The pool?"

"The whole house, darlin'," he corrected softly. "This place is so big, it goes on as much as a politician."

Bernadette smiled at the expression. "I love it."

"So do I." He grinned mischievously. "I need to check the arboretum. Want to come with me?"

"Arboretum?" Her attention focused on him again. "For birds?"

"Exotic ones."

"I wouldn't miss it," she said, following him out the back door toward what looked like a natural outcropping of rock—but wasn't. There was rock on three sides, but the final side and top were a wraparound formation of wire netting. Birds of various colors and sizes skipped from tree branch to rock to water pond. Their chirping sounded like music, their bright colors were a pleasure to the eye.

Cane took several photos to show where the rock had cracked at the base. Once he'd finished the roll, he pocketed the small but expensive camera.

"Hold this," he said, handing her the end of the tape measure as he walked away from her toward the corner of the house. With each measurement, he added figures to a diagram he'd drawn of the house and property. Then, with a few words to the elderly man who owned the house, they left, heading toward the next inspection. The first one had taken a little over two hours to complete.

"Are all those insureds that nice?" she asked, leaning back in the seat and staring out at the traffic around them—she hadn't realized that people in trucks could see into all the cars. . . .

"For the most part, people are nice. Just like any other business, you run into some real horse's asses on occasion." He glanced her way. "Excuse me, I meant to say, 'Some distraught and upset insureds.'"

Bernadette tried not to smile. "It must be hard to be nice when you've lost so many possessions."

"Darlin', if they were nice before the quake, they're usually nice now," Cane stated dryly. "If they were horse's—distraught before, they're usually carrying the same attitude now. The earthquake seems to bring out the best, and the worst, in everybody, depending on what they were before." He grinned at her. "Look at you. You were nice to begin with. You're nice now."

"Thanks. It's a compliment, isn't it?" She frowned. "I'm not sure, since I haven't thought a lot since the quake. I just keep going with the same attitude and hope that people recognize me for who I am. I'd hate to resemble a horse's—distraught person."

Cane grinned, but didn't say another word.

The rest of the day passed quickly for Bernadette. Every minute with Cane was fun. It was him and her against the mean ole earthquake. The Earthquake Crusaders, doing what they could to restore balance and harmony to others' lives.

She stared out the truck window as the sun began to set over the San Gabriel Mountains, then sink into the Pacific Ocean. "I love doing this," she declared, surprising herself that she'd said it aloud.

"I know the feeling. And you're a natural. You handle people so well."

"Or they handle me. I'm not sure which."

"Does it matter? Both you and the insured get something out of it. And both walk away feeling better."

"Not a bad combination," said softly, wondering why she'd never thought of this career before. "All I have to do is learn construction and I, too, can be a catastrophe insurance adjuster."

"Sorry, but you won't be breaking any glass ceilings. There are women out there already. My roommate, Cass, is a commercial adjuster, working with businesses and apartments."

Bernadette's heart dropped to her toes. "Roommate?" She hoped her voice didn't sound as tight as her throat felt.

"Yes. I'm living with two other adjusters. Cass and her brother, Reed. Cass just got her license, so she didn't come out here until we'd already rented our apartment. It's kinda cramped," he drawled, "but it's home for now."

"Have you known her long?" she finally managed, forcibly swallowing the lump in her throat.

"Since she was nothing but a willow twig in high school." There was pride in his voice.

"Reed, too?"

"Reed and I have hung around since we got our first job together. That same year Cass entered her first year of high school, and was a real pest. She wanted to go everywhere we went. It ended up that so long as we weren't on a date, she tagged along."

"That must have been nice," Bernadette said flatly, jealous of Cass's opportunity to be with Cane.

But he didn't seem to notice her irritation. "It was silly, but she quickly learned what was most on a young man's mind. In fact, by hanging around us she learned more about guys than any other girls her age." Cane's chuckle reverberated through the cab of the truck. "I'm still not sure whether that's good or bad. But it's too late to worry about it now."

"It must be cozy with the three of you in that small apartment. I thought my apartment was the largest one they had."

"It is, and it's larger than ours. When Cass came out, I gave her my room. I sleep on the couch and share a bathroom with Reed. It's the only way."

Relief flooded through her. "Where are you doing all the computer work?"

"In the living room. There's hardly room to sit and eat a meal, let alone work. But we manage."

Bernadette's mind whirled with possibilities. "Cane," she said slowly, her thoughts still jumbling in no apparent order. "Why don't you use my office for your work? Since you've asked for my help, and I certainly have the space, why don't you just share my study? It would certainly be easy, and that way I'd also have the files there when I need them."

Looking at his closed expression, she wondered if she'd stepped over some imaginary line of discretion. But then she straightened her spine. If what he'd said was true, she was offering him a more peaceful way to work.

Cane was silent so long, she wondered if perhaps he was ignoring her suggestion. Then, just as she was building up a head of indignant steam to let him know that she couldn't care less whether he answered or not, that she wasn't concerned whether he wanted to work with her or not, that she didn't care whether he lived or died, he finally spoke.

"Darlin', I'd be a fool to turn down an offer like that. What I'm not sure about is whether I should take advantage of you like that."

He looked over at her, his brows knitted together in a frown. "On the days I'm not scoping, I'm at the computer by six or seven in the morning and sometimes work until midnight. Won't that bother you?"

Breath whooshed from her lungs in relief. "I sleep like a rock. If I get tired, I'll go to bed and you can let yourself out."

He looked at her quizzically. "How can you trust me? You don't even know me."

She grinned. As if she'd need recommendations. "I know how much you've helped me. I know that your company trusts you. I haven't seen any sign of you not caring about your job. You seem to love it. In fact, I think you thrive on it. All that tells me is that you'll be a responsible, upstanding citizen because you want to keep your job." Her grin turned to laughter. "Besides, I know where your best friends live," she whispered conspiratorially.

His laughter joined hers. "So you do," he said.

"Besides, how do you know that I'm okay and not the newest mass murderer?" she asked. "Just because I'm a woman doesn't mean I'm safe."

"You're right. I'll have to introduce Reed and Cass to you so they'll know I'm in good hands."

"Sounds like it's in your own best interests," she said happily, leaning back and staring out the window once more. She gave a contented sigh.

Life was good.

"AND I TOLD HIM," Cassandra said. "'Mr. Paul, please leave your hands on the table and we'll continue to go through this estimate. But if they disappear, so do I.'"

Bernadette laughed along with Reed and Cane. Cassandra sat back and sipped on her chilled glass of wine, surveying the others for reaction.

Bernadette admired Cassandra's aplomb. She was smart, feminine, and making it in what looked very much like a man's career. That wasn't easy. Bernadette knew from her own experience just how tough it was.

"More wine?" Cane asked, holding up the bottle in readiness to pour.

Bernadette placed her hand over the top of the glass. She noticed he hadn't had any wine, either, preferring to drink a Texas beer from the can. "No more for me. I'm a working girl and have to get up early tomorrow."

"Did Cane wipe you out today?" Reed asked. "Just tell me the truth and I'll beat him up for you."

Cassandra laughed. "You wouldn't hurt a flea. Why, you've never been in a fight in your life, big brother. You've always had a silver tongue as a weapon."

Cane's deep chuckle reverberated in Bernadette's ears, waking every sensual nerve in her body. "How true. Why, he can't even kill time without getting a guilty conscience."

Bernadette wished she didn't have to leave, but she wasn't going to be able to stay here and still remain on her feet. As much as Cane affected her, she was almost too tired to do more than dream about what might have been. She stood and put her glass on the kitchen bar. "I'm sorry, guys, but Cane worked me so hard today that I have got to get to bed before I fall asleep standing up."

Cane stood, too, coming by her side. "I put her through the paces on adjusting today. She's been on her feet all day."

"When I wasn't in the car."

"Truck."

"Truck," she corrected herself. "It's a heck of a stress level you all work at."

"Don't we know it." Cass laughed. "I blame my brother for getting me into it. But too many days like the rough one today, and I'll be blaming Cane for it, too. After all, he made Reed join him."

Cane looked complacent. "I know misery when I see it. And who's more fun to take on a miserable trip through life than my best friend?"

"Remind me not to use you two for references," Reed observed, stacking a few of the extra plates. "With friends like you . . ."

Cane took Bernadette's elbow. "I'll argue with you later. Right now I'm walking this sweet sugar home."

"Uh-oh, Bernadette." Reed gave his friend an odd look. "Watch him. That's what he usually says before he goes in for the kill."

Bernadette felt a flush work its way up her neck to her cheeks. But she wasn't going to let their reaction affect her. "Don't worry. I bite."

Cane turned and faced his friends. "Reed? Take a long hike off a short pier," he stated calmly, then led Bernadette out of the apartment and quietly closed the door behind them.

"I'm sorry," he said. "I shouldn't have called you that. They were reminding me, friendly-like, of that fact."

Courage was all she had left. "Why? Because you have no designs on me?"

Holding her arm, he continued walking her around the courtyard and down the hall to the next wing. "Right. And you should be thankful about it. Besides, you're a client. Never get involved with a client."

"What a fine philosophy. But I think it might be too late for that piece of wisdom, since you've already hired me," she said dryly, ignoring her hurt feelings. "It sounds like I'm supposed to thank my lucky stars that I'm not attractive or sexy or smart enough to gain a man's attention." She was afraid to state that it was *his* attention she vied for.

They'd stopped in front of her door, and his dark brows rose incredulously. "Is that what you think? That you're not the sexiest thing to come along the flatlands in a long, long time?"

She nodded, trying to ignore the tempting scent of his after-shave. It pushed all her buttons. "That's what I think."

"Well, sweet thing, you're wrong."

She felt her breath whoosh out and knew that her toes were curling inside her tennis shoes.

"But I'm not going to take advantage of that fact. At least not while we're working together."

Turning, Bernadette slid the key in the lock and opened her door. Cane followed her down the hall into the dimly-lit living area. She dropped her purse on the bar stool and faced him. Even though she was tired, she didn't want him to leave. She wanted him to stay and— Her mind stopped at the thought of Cane making love to her. They didn't have that kind of relationship, no matter what her feelings were. "Thanks for today. And especially for tonight."

"Nothing to it."

"Your friends are terrific."

"They're the best," he said simply.

She couldn't think of anything else to delay him. "Well, it was a special evening and you're an excellent cook."

His grin was slow in coming. He stood directly in front of her, his muscle-hard body no more than six or so inches from hers. His gaze searched her face for something other than the compliment she gave him.

She could almost feel his shoulders relax. "Thank you. I love cooking, but not all the time. Those two don't seem to want to chip in when I'm tired."

She stared up at him. She wanted to feel his arms around her, holding her for just a moment. "At least they appreciate what you do."

"I'm lucky."

"And you've got a neat job, too." She wanted to feel his body pressed intimately against hers.

"I'm lucky." His voice lowered to a husky drawl.

"And now you've got someone to help you work." What she wanted was to delicately nibble on his bottom lip. What she needed was to have his lips conform to hers in a kiss that would rival their first one.

"I told you I was lucky."

She wanted the comfort of Cane but knew it wasn't to be. Her voice was low, finally saying what she'd only thought: "Damn."

"Damn," he echoed in a husky whisper.

Then his lips did what her heart wanted. His kiss was gentle at first, brushing against her lips like a soft butterfly wing. She inhaled and filled with the sexy scent of him, expelling her breath on a sigh.

Then he landed, drawing her mouth to his and taking her breath away.

Restraint didn't last for long. His arms encircled her waist, pulling her closer, molding her to his body the way his mouth molded her lips to his. He was in command. She knew it and so did he.

Her arms curled around his back and she held on for dear life as his tongue caressed hers.

Bernadette felt her heart quickening against Cane's chest. But it wasn't until she put her hands on his shoulders that she noticed his own heart was pumping just as furiously. Joy welled inside her as she realized that she was just as powerful an attraction to him as he was to her.

It was too soon when Cane finally pulled back. His warm breath caressed her cheek. "I want you, Bette. I want you in my bed. Now."

She smiled and let her hand drift to his throat, where a pulse beat heavily there. "It's Bernadette, and you don't have a bed."

"You do."

She rested her head against his chest. "Yes, I do. But are you going to be able to make love with me tonight and still work with me tomorrow?"

"Woman, you're tough," he said, with a heavy sigh.

She felt her spirits plummet, but found the courage to continue. "I want more than an occasional toss in the hay." It took everything she had to step out of his arms. The chilled night air circled around her and drifted between them. "I want much more."

His eyes narrowed. "What else?"

*Courage, Bernadette. This may be your one chance to explain. Don't blow it. Tell the truth.* She took a deep breath. "I want a long-term affair that suits both of us and makes us feel good about each other and ourselves."

Cane gave a low whistle. "Lady, you want too much. Especially from an old country boy like me."

Her soft, feminine gaze hardened to diamonds. "Don't pull the 'poor Texas boy' routine on me, Hurricane Mitchell. I know better than to believe it." She felt him pull away emotionally, but she wasn't willing to concede defeat. "You might not think this is a good idea now, but you could change your mind later. If you do, let me know."

"You're serious?"

"Very." Bernadette turned on the small light next to the couch, pretending to be calm and cool and collected—all the things she wasn't. "I would love to have a long-term affair with you. But I won't share your body with someone else, and I won't have less than your commitment to me for the length of time we're together."

She turned and stared at him, silently demanding an answer.

The very definite gleam in his eyes told her he admired her frankness. It also said that he still wanted her. Those very thoughts kept her mind warmed even while she felt chilled without his nearness.

"I won't be staying here." His tone was warning enough. "When this job is over, I'll be heading to the next catastrophe or back to Texas."

Although she didn't want to think about it, she already knew that. "But that's not the point, is it, Cane? We're talking about the here-and-now." She perched on an arm of her overstuffed leather couch. "I'm not the kind for a one-night stand, and you might enjoy having a steady partner while you're here."

"Why?"

She shrugged, unwilling to meet his eyes any longer for fear that the longing in hers would show. "Just a thought."

"Are you giving me an ultimatum?" His voice was distant, his chilliness even more so.

She shook her head in denial. "I'm offering a suggestion that might benefit both of us. If you don't think so, then we'll just continue working the way we are and no hurt feelings. If you decide otherwise . . . well—" she shrugged "—let me know and we can discuss it further."

A small grin tugged at his mouth. "What would there be to discuss?"

Bernadette hadn't thought that far ahead. In fact, she had stunned herself that she'd gotten this far in the conversation. She'd never been this forward in her life! But if there was one thing the earthquake had taught her, it was that life could change at a moment's notice. Life was to be lived now and if she wanted something badly enough, she'd better find the courage to go after it.

She slipped her hands under her, not wanting to let him know what a toll this conversation was taking on her nerves. "That's up to you."

"Thanks for letting me make some of the decisions in this discussion."

Bernadette tried to keep from smiling, but the corners of her mouth turned up anyway. "You're welcome."

Cane kept staring at her. Suddenly she wished she'd never found enough nerve to bring up the topic. So much for reaching out and grabbing life with both hands. Instead, Cane probably thought she'd done this a thousand times before. What was the matter with her?

She stood, anxious to close the door and be by herself. She wanted to end this embarrassment. "Look, I'm sorry. This was a bad idea I didn't even think through and should have." She walked past him to the door and opened it slightly, then rested her hand on the knob while she tried once more to explain. "It's all wrong. I'm sorry. Let's not think about this. Years from now, we'll both remember this as a joke." Didn't she wish! Right now she wouldn't have minded in the least if a tidal wave had come up and swept her offshore, never to return to Glendale.

The silence between them lasted the longest minute of Bernadette's life. Then, suddenly, Cane Mitchell strode down the hallway toward her. But when he reached her side, instead of striding out the door, he placed his hand flat on its surface and closed it tightly.

"I believe we have business in the other room?" he said softly.

She swallowed hard. "I don't think so."

"Against the rules, Ms. Conrad. You made the offer, and you can't withdraw it until I reject it." His voice was smooth and low, filled with a sexiness that every nerve and muscle in Bernadette's body responded to. "And I'm not going to."

"You mean . . . ?" She couldn't think of a thing to say. Her nerves were tight and anxious again. Strange how her tiredness had disappeared once they were alone together. . . .

"That's exactly what I mean." His head bent down to hers. "I accept your offer and the terms you set out. Now—" he lowered his head until his lips brushed hers tantalizingly as he spoke "—please be quiet while I decide whether to make love to you in your bed, or here in the hallway."

Bernadette did as she was told only because she couldn't have moved if she'd wanted to. Her legs had turned to jelly....

# 5

CANE'S KISS WASN'T LIKE this morning's. It was harder, more purposeful. He evoked emotions she'd never experienced before, and she held on to him for dear life.

Her fingers crept around his neck, losing themselves in his thick hair, as she held on for all her worth. He made her dizzy, his touch bringing her to heights she'd never thought she would find. This was what she wanted—what she had dreamed of all her life. But she had never expected this wonderful feeling to be real. Being enclosed in Cane's arms was the very stuff that dreams were made of—especially *her* dreams.

It wasn't until his hands slid down her hips and thighs in order to sling her into his arms that she found the strength to pull away from his kiss. "Wha—"

"Shh," he said, pressing another quick kiss on the curve of her neck. "I've always wanted to do this. Now's my chance to look like a he-ro. Besides, you're so tiny."

Her laughter was low, muffled against his hard shoulder. "Rhett!" she exclaimed softly in her best Southern imitation. She felt positively feminine and yielding and wonderful. Unable to find the words to describe the wonderful feeling, she purred instead, in a sound that came from deep in her throat.

He carried her into her room and stood her on the floor beside her bed. Her eyes, as round as saucers, watched while he slipped his shirt over his head, then undid the belt and zipper on his dark pants.

Soon he was naked and everything she'd guessed about his build was confirmed. She'd known he had a beautiful chest, but the rest of him was just as hard and male and whipcord lean. He was gorgeous.

He slipped her khaki pants down around her hips. She shifted, and the pants came off. Then he scooted her T-shirt up, lifting it over her head. As Bernadette edged out of the sleeves, the clasp of her bra was quickly unsnapped and she felt the freedom of release—then reveled in the heat of his hands as he cradled her breasts. His head dipped as he leaned down and took her nipple in his mouth, circling his hot, wet tongue around the areola and sending flames searing through her body. Bernadette felt her legs weaken, barely holding her up.

Her hands dug into his shoulders, her head dropping forward to watch his head as he kissed a trail lower on her belly. She gasped as he sought out her inner folds and gently caressed her, touching her in the most intimate way possible. A low moan forced its way from her parted lips and she felt her legs buckle. But Cane was there, ready, helping her stretch out on the bed.

Then he was lying next to her, his weight a perfect counterpoint to her slenderness. He searched, found and kissed all the sensitive spots on her neck and shoulder. A soft moan escaped her throat, but Cane caught it in his mouth and returned it.

His body covered hers like a blanket and she reveled in the weight. Her own breath came in short wisps, caressing his skin as much as he soothed and warmed hers. And in doing so, he gave her unbelievable pleasure.

Her breath caught in her throat as the pleasure built to a climax. He moaned and she recognized that Cane was experiencing the same wonderful sensations.

Their eyes closed, they remained entwined. She smiled and stroked his back and neck in a loving motion. He gently kissed the corner of her mouth and she parted her lips.

"I gather you're pleased?" he asked, his voice barely a whisper.

Her smile broadened. "You gather correctly, Rhett."

"Then I don't need any more practice?"

Bernadette's eyes opened. Cane was staring down at her, wearing an endearing grin even larger than her own. "Absolutely not," she said, smiling.

"I'm loving every minute of being with you." She stroked the hair at his temples. "Thank you."

He grinned again, showing his dimples. "You're very welcome."

Her lashes fluttered. Her brain craved sleep even as she wished she could stare at him forever.

Cane reached over and pulled the afghan from the bottom of the bed, covering them both. Bernadette curled into him, sharing the heat his body radiated. His chest hair tickled her nose and she tilted her head sideways, leaving a small trail of kisses where her mouth had been.

"We'll just relax for a few minutes, then I'll go," he promised huskily, his arms tightening around her before beginning a gentle stroking.

"Yes," she replied, her eyes closing again. "But not yet." She placed her lips against his shoulder, then cuddled against him. "Wait a while."

Seconds later, she was asleep.

Cane stared down at the woman who was curled so trustingly in his arms and he wondered if he was in heaven or just plain stupid. It had to be one or the other. God had never before given him this much happiness and contentment at once. This couldn't be right.

Ever since he could remember, he'd thought there was something—some key ingredient—missing from his life, but he'd never quite put his finger on what that particular ingredient was. He'd always imagined that others knew what it was and possessed it, but not him. Never him. Now, for the first time, he held a very special woman in his arms and suddenly felt complete. It was wrong. He didn't deserve to feel this content. He knew it; and if he wasn't careful, she'd know it, too. Better to keep this wonderful feeling a secret.

Tiredness overcame him, wrapping his mind in a foglike trance. He blinked, still staring down at her soft form and face. A lethargic relaxation invaded every muscle. He pulled the pillow down and rested his head next to hers. Placing a light kiss on each brow, then one on the tip of her nose, he closed his eyes. Just for a little while he wanted to pretend that this was a natural and normal state of affairs for Cane Mitchell, and that he would go on this way forever....

Bernadette awakened to a light snore in her ear. It took her a moment to orient herself. She was naked, lying across the bed, covered with an afghan she'd made years ago. And sleeping next to her was Cane.

She tensed. His hand rested possessively on her waist, his fingers curled lightly into her flesh. She tried to figure out how it made her feel, and then realized that of all the emotions that filled her, she felt comforted most. And happy. And contented. And satisfied. An entire list of words came to mind without her even trying.

She smiled, then closed her eyes and fell gently asleep again, still curled securely in Cane's arms.

But when sun filtered through the half-closed drapes and showered her wall with light, Bernadette knew it was time to wake up. She also knew instantly that something was different.

Cane was gone.

Hoping it was her imagination, she rolled over only to find a pillow laid lengthwise against her back. He'd been considerate enough to know that she'd miss his warm body next to hers.

"Damn him," she muttered, pulling herself up and sitting on the edge of the bed. She refused to admit that the disappointment swamping her invaded her every movement. They had been so good together, from working in tandem, to laughing, to making love....

The coffeepot timer beeped five times, telling her that fresh coffee was made and ready for her to pour.

She felt a depressed lethargy flow over her and admitted that she had no bone to pick with Cane for leaving. She had brazenly invited—probably demanded, by his standards—Cane Mitchell into her bed. And now she was surprised that he'd run out on her? *Get a life!* she told herself. She'd made a mistake, and now was the time to pay for it. Bad judgment was bad judgment.

Maybe next time she'd think twice about luring a handsome man she cared too much for into her bed. It was much easier to remain celibate than go through this self-inflicted agony. She stood and walked past the mirror toward the bathroom. "Like I do this all the time," she told her reflection in the mirror.

Bernadette stopped near the doorway to the living room. She heard the faint sound of a keyboard being punched. Her nerves tightened and hummed. Cane was still here in her apartment. If her hearing was right, he was on the computer in the office.

She reached around the bathroom door and grabbed her robe from the hook. Slipping her arms into the sleeves, she glanced quickly into the mirror. Tousled hair, a light smudge of mascara under each eye and no blush. She looked terrible.

Cane's voice came from bedroom door. "Darlin'? Can I get you a cup of coffee?"

"Please," she called from behind the partially closed bathroom door. "I'll be right out."

She pushed the door closed with her toe, then turned on the faucet. With alarming speed, she washed her face and brushed her teeth. How did the movies get away with the glamorizing myth that women looked beautiful when they woke up in the morning? Any self-respecting woman over the age of twenty had more makeup on the pillow than on her face. And Bernadette was no exception. What little makeup she'd worn yesterday was gone, and a pale face greeted her instead.

She ran a brush through her hair, took a deep breath and came out of the bathroom at the same time Cane walked into the bedroom with an extra cup in his hand. He was dressed in the clothing he'd worn yesterday—black jeans and a white shirt with an insurance emblem on the pocket. But unlike her, he looked just as neat and clean this morning as he had yesterday."

"You're dressed," she accused.

"And you're not." Cane stopped midway across the room and stared down at her, his eyes glowing with admiration. "Damn, but you look beautiful."

She smiled self-consciously. "You're a liar, but don't stop now."

Cane held out her cup. "And you're almost as effervescent and charming this morning as you were last evening."

She felt awkward and ill at ease. She thought of the night before, when their bodies had been lovingly entwined, the image flashing through her mind. She felt a blush work its way up her neck. "Thank you. So are you." She took the mug without letting her eyes meet his.

"Hope you don't mind, but I've been looking around. You've got a nice office setup," he said. The subject change was welcome, to ground she was more familiar with and could handle. "One of everything you could possibly need."

"That's my business, remember?" she told him, sipping on her very hot coffee. "A secretarial service has to have that 'setup,' or clients will go elsewhere."

"I know, but it's still nice to see. I've needed some of that equipment and just haven't gotten it yet." She followed him as he walked into the kitchen. He refreshed his own cup of coffee and Bernadette could smell soap. He must have taken a shower at his place and returned here—all while she was sleeping.

She reached for a cube of ice and dropped it into her cup. "How long have you been up?"

"Long enough to put the estimating program in your computer. It's ready to operate now. I'll show you how to run it later this morning. You've got so many other programs in there, I don't think you'll have a problem learning this one."

"Great!" she said with a false smile. "I'm looking forward to it."

"But right now, you'd like me to leave you alone so you can get on with your life. I mean . . . dressing." His tone held a hint of laughter.

"I wouldn't say that," she replied, suddenly feeling better. "I'm thinking it, but I certainly wouldn't say it aloud. It's bad manners."

His laugh was wonderful and sexy. "I don't blame you. I've interfered with your private time enough. I'm going back to my apartment and have a good long talk with myself over wearing out my welcome. Call me when you feel like looking through the program. Until then, I'll stay out of your hair." His gaze caressed her freshly brushed hair. "Although I'd love to get lost in it again," he said softly, reminding her of last night. He reached out and touched a tendril that popped from behind her ear. "It's so silky and soft. Just like the rest of you."

Bernadette blushed.

Cane stepped closer to her and stared down with eyes that said more than words ever could. "I'm not sure how to say I thought last night was wonderful without stepping on your toes. So I'll say it straight out and hope you understand enough to put the right embellishments on my simple thought."

His hands touched her shoulders lightly, his index fingers soothing the side of her neck so sweetly she wanted to arch into his palm.

Instead, she smiled. He'd just put the sunshine back in her heart. "Thank you. I feel the same way."

"I'm glad I'm not alone." He bent close and kissed her forehead. The scent of his after-shave underlined their intimacy of last night. "Thanks again."

She couldn't discuss this. All those feelings were still too close. Too personal. Too ... She was afraid she'd say something that would scare him away before she had a chance to explain. Instead, she changed the subject. "I think we need to pay attention to business and not make what happened the focus of our times together." What in heaven's name was she saying? She wanted nothing more than to be caught in Cane's arms and made love to for hours! "After all, we've got plenty of work."

A strange look came into his eyes and he took a step back. "Sure. Why don't you just call the apartment when you're ready to go through the program? Then I'll come back. Meanwhile, I've still got some calls to make and a few files I need to set up."

"Of course," she said, pretending she was as calm and cool as he was. Inside, her nerves were a frayed mess. The man of her dreams was leaving and she didn't know what to say. "Thank you. I had a wonderful time." A wonderful time! What an insane thing to say!

"So did I." He twisted the doorknob and stood in the doorway. "Talk to you soon."

And then he disappeared into the hall, closing the door behind him.

Bernadette stood in the center of her kitchen, her face still on fire.

If Cane Mitchell had anything to do with her after this morning's fiasco, it would be a miracle. She not only looked like a worn-out piece of womanhood, she sounded like a witless wonder!

Her heart hurt most of all. She'd been alone and feeling numb for so long, that for just a little while she realized what it was to be alive again. To feel her heart pounding and her pulse running swiftly told her that she'd been asleep too long. This was life. Occasional embarrassment and hurt. Lots of laughter and conversation. Love and loss and feelings! Those were the ingredients that proved she'd been a part of life all this time but had forgotten to live. To feel again the energy of living was exhilarating.

And if she had to take some of the bad with the good, it would be all right. She'd been sleepwalking through this life for far too long.

Thank you, Hurricane Mitchell.

She just hoped he was appreciative enough of her thanks to stick around and say, "Welcome."

CANE STRODE DOWN the corridor toward his apartment. He cursed himself for being six kinds of fool and then some. First he'd done the stupid thing by taking Bernadette to her own bed. Then he'd had the gall to fall asleep and spend the night there. But worse was that he'd left her, cleaned up and then gone back to greet her waking form. What had he been hoping for? That she would take him back to bed and spend the morning making mad, passionate love? That she would greet him with open arms and a kiss on the cheek, as if she awakened with him beside her every day of her life?

He slipped the key in the lock and opened the apartment door. The place was quiet except for muffled street noises drifting through the open patio doors. Both Reed and Cassandra had made appointments to scope all day today. Without them here, it was an empty, corporate apartment that he called home.

He contrasted it with Bernadette's cozy place. The two apartments were as different as silk and a sow's ear. And his "own" room wasn't even his own. It was a living area where he and his friends worked on computers or sat on the couch and watched TV until lights-out. Then he threw down a sheet and called it a bed. Not even a magician would have the nerve to label it a "bedroom."

Cane paced around the apartment like a caged wolf, wanting to strike out at something or someone, but unsure whom to blame for his unsettled feelings. He finally had to admit that this emotion was his own fault.

He'd had a tiny taste of normalcy—of home and love and caring—and he craved more. That small taste of heaven had upset his equilibrium and made him frustrated with what little he had.

He wanted to run away from Bernadette—right after he held her so preciously she would never want to leave him.

He stopped in front of the mirror hanging in the hall. "You're crazy, buddy," he stated in disgust. "You deserve it if the woman never called you again. In fact, you'd both be better off."

Cane felt as if he was getting in over his head. He wasn't even sure what "over his head" meant anymore. He should have hated feeling this way about a woman.

When the phone rang, Cane grabbed it.

"Cane?" Bernadette's voice filled his ear with softness and a vibration he felt all the way down to his toes. "I'm awake and dressed and ready to tackle learning a new program."

He clenched the phone. Everything in him wanted to run away.

"Cane?"

"Fine," he said curtly. "I'll be right down."

When he arrived at her door, he'd already cursed himself five times over for not running. She wasn't in his league. He wished he could think of a way to be with her more often, but she was far above the type of women he usually—

The door opened and Bernadette stood in front of him wearing a cropped pale blue sweater and matching shorts. She looked like a sexy poster woman. Just the thought made his blood boil. So did her sweet smile.

"Hey, there," she said breezily. "I've just made fresh coffee if you want some."

"Thanks, but I think I'm coffeed out." He stepped inside.

"Fine." She closed the door and started down the hall.

"What did you do with the extra bedroom?" Cane asked, following her.

"What could I do with it? For now, I turned it into a shrine in honor of my son." She went into the study and pulled an extra chair up to her computer desk. "But next week I'm placing an ad in the paper for a roommate. Someone who can cook and keep me entertained enough so that I won't feel those blessed aftershocks."

She sat in front of the computer and Cane sat beside her. "I can do that," he said quietly, astounding himself as well as Bernadette.

"What?" She looked surprised.

"Rent a room."

"Why would you be thinking of renting a room, Cane?"

"Why not?"

"You already have an apartment."

"I don't have a bedroom, and that's what you've got empty. I sleep on a couch and share Reed's bathroom. It's not handy. While you, Wonder Woman, have an extra bedroom with a bath attached. And you're not using either one."

"Are you serious?"

He pretended to open a file and study it. He couldn't look at her and see her lack of support for such a crazy idea. "Never more so." He looked up, intending to write off his words with a shrug that spelled out how little he cared what her answer was. But he was stopped cold by her expression.

"Well." She stared at him, a grin slowly forming that she was sure told him just how pleased she was. But if that didn't, the warm gleam in her eyes underlined it. "Sold," she said.

He tried not to jump up and shout. "Good. When can I move in?"

Bernadette tilted her head in thought. "Why not today?"

"This afternoon?"

She nodded. Her heart beat quickly, like a happy bird. "After you teach me the rudiments of this program, so I can practice while you're getting your stuff together."

"Fair enough."

She opened the program and Cane began showing her the starting commands that she would need to maneuver. Time flew by as he explained the processes and procedures he followed to document an insured's file and estimate. He sat slightly behind her. She pretended to be paying complete attention to his notes and instructions, but all the while, Bernadette was completely aware of Cane's knee touching hers and his warm breath on her neck as he leaned forward.

She tried to keep her mind on the program but the image of them sleeping together, lying together, making love, kept replaying in her mind over and over. If she continued to replay it, her face would flush scarlet and then he would know what was on her mind. So she concentrated hard on what Cane was telling her about the estimate program.

"Think you can do it?" Cane finally asked, leaning back and stretching out his long legs.

"I'm sure with practice I'll get the hang of it."

"Good. Then try entering this file information into the computer. I brought it with me earlier this morning. While you do that, I'll start getting my gear together."

"Fine," she said, pretending she was studying the loss report sheet.

Cane stood and tucked his shirt back into his jeans. "Need anything else?"

"Not right now," she said.

"Be right back, little lady." He left the study and went down the hall.

Bernadette opened the file and placed it next to the computer, but she never went any further. Her heart was racing, her hands felt clammy. Her breath came in short, shallow wisps.

Over and over she told herself to concentrate on what she was doing, but it was nearly impossible. Cane was moving in. Cane was moving in!

She didn't know where to begin, what to do. Since her husband died, she hadn't lived with anyone other than her son. Sharing a life with another grown-up was so long ago, she didn't even remember. Besides, this wasn't the same time or the same man. And she wasn't the same naive Bernadette, for that matter.

What would she do, what should she ask for? Should she cook and clean for two, or have him chip in on the cleaning? Should he help pay for the food? Could she wear a robe or would she have to get dressed before she left her room in the morning? A thousand questions bounced around her head. She continued to stare at the papers in the file, the numbers blurring as she listened to a slightly off-key tune whistled in the other room.

The door opened and she heard Cane's whistle turn louder as he began putting his things away in the spare bedroom.

He seemed so casual about it. She wished she could be that way. While she worried about two hundred different things, he probably didn't have a care in the world....

CANE STOOD in the center of the room and wondered if he could have lost his mind as easily as he lost his socks. What in the hell was he doing! Was he insane? Was he so besotted he was crazy?

He knew the answers, he just didn't like them. He hadn't lost his mind, he was just a conniving SOB working toward his goal—the goal of getting into the life and home of a woman he wanted to be with. He wasn't insane, just damned sneaky. And yes, he was besotted. For all the good it would do him.

Bernadette Conrad was not the type of woman to be interested in him for long. She was sweet and classy. And she was so kind, she would offer her home to anyone she trusted.

That was the problem.

When it came to women, Hurricane Mitchell wasn't trustworthy.

He was born of a Galveston hooker and a man who could barely stand up most of the time. In fact, when his old man did stand, all he could do was slap, hit or punch whoever was within arm-swinging distance. Cane learned at a young age not to get within that range. He also learned never to demand attention from his mother when she was "busy." He'd grown up street-tough, world-weary and without ever really connecting with anyone.

It certainly wasn't the way Bernadette had been raised. If she knew anything of the seamy side of life, it was by getting lost and accidentally driving through the "wrong" part of town. She had no idea of the hidden horrors that walked the streets at night or played on the waterfront at any time of day.

And that was probably what he liked most about her—that sense of innocence, of cleanness. Her optimism about life wasn't tainted by the dirt and scum that layered his past.

Her smile was pure sunshine, her heart giving.

And he wanted all of it he could get. "Dammit, Mitchell, you've got a right to some happiness!" he muttered to the image of himself in the bathroom mirror. He heard the words, but he didn't believe them.

Instead of looking himself in the eye, he had to turn away.

What he was doing, his conscience told him, was tainting that which was good and fine and sweet.

And he needed that goodness from Bernadette as much as he needed air.

Straightening his back, he whistled purposefully as he left the room and strolled toward the office area.

His decision had been made. For a little while he was going to pretend that he was just as nice and ordinary as anybody else. He was going to enjoy that pretense, too.

Instead of feeling soiled, with Bernadette's help, he was going to feel clean and regular and normal. In return, he would try not to hurt her in the process. . . .

# 6

BERNADETTE DID HER BEST to keep her grin from bursting into full-blown laughter. She almost succeeded.

Cane sat next to her, concentrating on the keyboard. His fingers moved over the keys in a slow, haphazard pattern of hunt-and-peck. How he kept up the pace for very long, she'd never know. If it were her, her index fingers would be cramped. He'd somehow managed to keep at it this way for the past two hours without stop. Bernadette just sat back and watched in awe and wonder.

"There," he muttered in satisfaction, tapping a final period.

"Where?" she asked, finally glancing at his hands instead of the computer screen. They were strong hands.

"There." He pointed to the screen. "It's done." He looked at her, a grin as boyish as could be. "Think you can do it?"

"I can do anything you can do, Mister," she said, a touch of teasing superiority lacing her tone. "Anything except type with two fingers."

"You're jealous of my dexterity."

"I'm not." She grinned. "But I am in awe of it. I've never seen anything quite so . . . amazing."

"Thank you," he said, nodding his head in a bow. "I'm not only good, I'm great."

"Do you always do things the hard way?"

"That's not harder than learning how to undo a lifetime of typing don'ts. Take my word for it. I've tried before. Besides, I'm damn good."

Bernadette scooted her chair toward his. "Don't get carried away," she warned. "I'm better. I'm just not familiar with your line of work or I'd be three times faster."

"You don't know that."

"Yes, I do."

Cane sighed audibly. "All right. My secret's out. I'm really fast for a lousy typist."

Bernadette chuckled. "Isn't it wonderful and cleansing for the soul when we tell the truth?" She patted him on the back. "I'm so proud of you."

"Shut up and start typing," Cane grumbled, reaching for the next file and handing it to her. "You're my slave for the day. Get working."

"Watch it, big boy," she soothed. "Or you'll find yourself out in the street before you can even find out if you like the 'ness' of the bed."

"'Ness'?"

"Right. Like, firmness, softness, bounciness, et cetera." Bernadette clicked the mouse and opened the first file she was going to work on.

"Oh, you're right." He was quiet for a moment, watching her. "I wouldn't want to have you lose your concentration now. Especially since I want you in more than one place."

Her tongue curled to the outside of her lip in concentration. "What?"

Cane stood and leaned down to whisper in her ear. "I want you in more than one place. I want you in front of the computer at work and in front of me when we make love."

Bernadette's hands dropped to her lap. "Cane, we can't make love again."

Cane's brows lifted and the light went out of his eyes. "No? Why?"

"Because it's not right. Not if we're going to work together."

"I'm not sure I understand." Cane stepped back to the doorway, hands on his hips as he stared down at her. He made her so uncomfortable that she squirmed in her seat. "Let me get this straight. You're saying that as long as we're living together and working together, we can't make love?"

She wasn't sure why, but she decided to stick to her guns. "Something like that."

"That means that if I go back to my crowded apartment with my two friends, where I don't have a bed or a bath, you'll let me back in your bed again?"

"It wouldn't be a business partnership anymore." It was a feeble protest at best.

He turned around and headed toward the door. "Okay. I'll be busy moving all day."

Bernadette swiveled around. "Moving?"

"Yes. I'm moving back to the apartment down the hall—the one without a bed and bath."

She was totally astounded. "Why?"

"So I can be in your bed, making love to you in the dark of night—or as dark a night as the big lights of Los Angeles will allow."

Bernadette leaned back and crossed her arms over her chest. She stared up at him. "You'd do that for me?"

"I'm not that unselfish. I'm doing that for me," he corrected softly but with a firmness that showed his strength of will. "It's what I want. Making love to you is too good. I can always find another secretary, but not another you in my arms."

Her shoulders slumped but her smile was firmly and rightfully in place. "Then I guess I'll have to give in. Occasionally."

"Occasionally?"

She nodded. "As in once in a while. Now and then. Periodically."

"As in tonight?"

That was the signal she needed to give in. Why was she holding out when what she wanted more than anything else was to be in his arms? "As in tonight."

His smile was smug. "Good." He turned away. "In that case, I'll finish unpacking."

"Good." She turned toward the computer. "In that case I'll finish working."

"Holler at me if you need help," he called over his shoulder. "Otherwise just look at the stuff in my computer."

"After I finish. Right now I want to see how much of my lessons I retained."

"Concentrate, concentrate, concentrate," he called, laughter tinging his deep voice.

But she couldn't concentrate much. Every other image in her mind was of the two of them making love in her bed. When it happened again, there would be no time restraint, no concern about being caught in a compromising situation, not even a problem with tiredness. The way she felt right now, Bernadette didn't stand a chance of catching any sleep for at least a week....

She heard muffled sounds of drawers and doors opening and closing and a slightly off-key humming as she typed away. Every keystroke she made, every thought she had about work was exchanged for one to do with Cane. In her mind's eye she could see him wandering around the bedroom, putting things away— intimate things like socks. Underwear. Shaving items and toothbrush and toothpaste.

Bernadette swallowed hard. This wasn't the time to even think such thoughts.

Bending her head, she forced herself to begin the process of learning how many files she could enter without getting too messed up. Then she could check them against the information in Cane's computer and see how she was doing. If he could do it, so could she.

When she next glanced at her watch, the late-afternoon sun was pouring a ribbon of light over her lap. Several hours had flown by. She was stiff and exhausted. Raising her hands above her head, Bernadette arched her back to ease some of the kinks, then stretched her arms in front of her.

Callused hands came from behind and stroked her shoulders and neck, kneading her flesh just enough to relax that part of those muscles while the rest of her sang with a new kind of tension—tension because Cane was near. She curved her head around to her shoulder.

"How does that feel?" he asked, his strong fingers kneading gently at the base of her neck.

She dropped her head forward and closed her eyes. "I'm going to make you stop that in a month or so."

He eased his fingers through her hair and massaged her scalp and around her ears and temples. She couldn't contain the satisfied moan that passed her lips.

His strong hands returned to her shoulders and back, soothing, pushing and kneading her muscles until she thought she'd melt like butter.

His hands were magical, his voice hypnotic. "Why don't you lie down for a few minutes while I finish dinner? You could use the break."

"You?" She opened her eyes and looked over her shoulder. "Cook dinner?"

"Don't forget that I'm an excellent cook, even if dinner is only pesto with a salad." He ran his fingers down her spine. "Do you like pesto?"

"What kind of nuts did you use?"

"Pine nuts and cashews. It's all you had on hand."

"I love it." She leaned forward to give him better access. "Can I help?"

"No. I like to travel around the kitchen without worrying who I'm going to step on or bump into." His hands traveled to her temples, rubbing lightly in a circular motion, his fingers tangled erotically in her hair. "You can either lie down or rest on the couch and watch the news."

"How long will it be?"

"Half an hour."

She leaned her head back and rested against Cane's firm stomach. Opening her eyes, she stared up at him. His hands rested warmly on her shoulders as he waited for her answer. She didn't want to admit that it took several minutes just to remember the question!

"I'll rest," Bernadette finally replied. Pulling away, she stood and closed the last file she'd worked on. She wished she hadn't been so quick to lose his grasp. Everywhere he touched and stroked, he spread a delicious, languid heat.

When she turned around, Cane was still standing behind her chair, hands on his lean hips as he watched her with a hooded gaze. "What? Is my slip showing?"

His answering grin as he looked up and down her slim form made her heart do a flip-flop. "I'm just enjoying the scenery. And anticipating the hidden scenes."

She turned back and stacked the files neatly. He wasn't going to get her rattled and he wasn't going to get away with sexist conversation, either. It was time to warn him who was in charge. "Well, don't get carried away, buddy boy. When it comes to what I choose and choose not to do, I still call the shots."

"And don't we all know it," he murmured. "But that doesn't keep me from thinking about it, darlin'."

When she turned around, he was gone. Damn him! He was the most exasperating, sexual man she'd ever been around! And she didn't like it one bit! She had gone for so long without desire coursing through her veins. It had been such a long time since she'd felt so sensually aroused.

Cane had come along and wakened things in her that she hadn't known still existed.

As much as she enjoyed being in Cane's arms, however, a part of her didn't want to be reminded that she was a sexual woman. She resented having that side of her revived, especially by a man who apparently thought her brain wasn't half as attractive, her personality half as important as the way she turned him on!

Damn the man!

She strode into her room and closed the door. With a muffled groan, she plopped across the foot of the bed. Her anger disappeared as quickly as her eyes closed.

When she awoke, it was to the scent of freshly peeled garlic. She rolled over and opened her eyes. Cane stood at the side of the bed, his hands at his sides. His mouth was turned up in a soft grin. He looked sexier than anyone had a right to look.

And twice as sexy as she felt.

"Hi, there, sleepyhead. I wasn't going to bother you but I got kinda worried," he drawled in that East Texas accent she was beginning to miss when she didn't hear it. "I didn't know if you died, got sick, or needed help."

Bernadette rolled over and sat up, straightening her top as she did so. "Why?"

"You've been asleep for almost two hours."

"I have?" She looked at her watch. "Good grief, you're right." Her eyes widened and her gaze showed her dismay. "And you said dinner would be in thirty minutes. Did I ruin it?"

Cane chuckled. "Ruin pesto? Not as long as there's a microwave." He bent down and placed a light kiss on her forehead that touched her down to her toenails. "Brush your hair and I'll serve the plates."

Bernadette did as she was told, quickly brushing her hair, then wanting to cry when she looked in the mirror and saw a bedspread crease crossing one cheek. Hot water helped, but didn't take away the indentation entirely. She could stay hidden in the bedroom until the mark went away, but she had the feeling Cane wouldn't allow it. She could hear the kitchen sounds now as he heated up the meal they were supposed to have eaten hours ago.

Her heart beat erratically as she walked into the living area. Cane was here, in her home. Wonderful, sexy, vibrant, good-looking Cane was here with her. Living with her!

She found it hard to believe, harder to live through. She also found herself more shy than she'd ever felt before.

What did she do now? Act casual? Apologize again? Help? She felt she knew him in so many ways, but didn't know him at all in others. With every day that passed, she would get to know him better, but that didn't help tonight.

Cane entered the dining area with two plates in his hands. He set them down on the already-laid table and pulled out her chair.

With as much aplomb as she could muster, Bernadette took the seat and waited for him to join her before she placed her napkin in her lap.

"Tell me about yourself, Hurricane Mitchell."

Cane poured red wine into her glass, then reached for his beer can. "What is it you're lookin' for, sweetlin'?"

Bernadette wound several strands of spaghetti around her fork. "Anything. Everything. There's a lot I don't know about you."

"Fair enough." Cane took a sip of his wine and stared into the kitchen/bar area. "I came from a very poor family who gave me up when I was very young. I moved from foster home to foster home. Then I got into some trouble and decided it was time to straighten up my act. I did. And here I am."

It was the volumes he didn't say that broke her heart. Bernadette cleared her throat. "You said you didn't have any children." She twirled the pasta around her fork. "Have you ever been married?"

Cane nodded, swallowed some pesto and spoke. "Yes. But it was as unfair to her as it was to me. We married because we both thought it was the thing to do. Our friends were all doing it. We didn't have the slightest idea what went into a marriage, so we pretended nothing did. The marriage died a painful but natural death."

Bernadette's heart ached for his loss. "How sad."

"How normal," Cane corrected. He waved toward the patio—and the world. "I don't know if you've noticed, but the world is filled with unhappy people. Rich people, poor people, ordinary people. They're all unhappy for whatever reason suits their fancy. We weren't the exception—we were the norm."

"Everyone has problems adjusting to having someone in their lives," she protested. "There are morals and opinions to be combined, compromises to be made. And a certain amount of wonderful taking-for-granted goes on in every relationship. That doesn't ordinarily run into being unhappy. Most people choose to be unhappy or happy. Life goes on regardless of their choices. That's why it's so nice to know what to expect from your partner—or at least assume you do."

"Take my word for it, there's nothing wonderful about being taken for granted," Cane stated dryly. "I've been there all my life. It's just one step away from being abused."

"Then it's not the right kind of being taken for granted." Bernadette placed her fork on her plate and leaned forward to explain. "There's nothing like being taken for granted when it's right."

"Example." Cane was demanding. She could see his impatience. He wanted to shoot down her theory. But she also saw his interest in the concept.

"It's a wonderful feeling to take for granted that your partner will be worried if you don't show up when you say you will. Or to know that he or she doesn't like bell peppers in his food. Or that he'll say a certain phrase every evening before turning off the TV—or do certain things that become ritual between you both."

She smiled as some of the old memories flooded her. "It used to be wonderful to know that my husband would always say, 'Sorry, but I know my wife. She won't see a war film.' He took it for granted because I cringe at bombs going off in movies. I don't care for sudden sounds. I never corrected him because I liked his trying to read my feelings about what I liked and didn't like. It meant he was trying to keep in touch with me."

"Did you ever correct him?" Cane took another sip of his wine.

"Yes. Every time he made a wrong assumption. When he thought I loved sweet chocolate and bought it all the time, I had to show him the difference between semisweet and sweet. When he took for granted that I didn't want him to have a night out with the guys, I had to explain that I occasionally needed that same time to spend by myself."

"Lucky man."

"Yes, he was. But so was I. Only because we worked at it." She sat back in her chair and picked up her fork again, taking another bite of her dinner and tasting it for the first time. Her brows rose. "Great pesto."

"Thanks."

Silence stretched between them. Bernadette chastised herself for going into some kind of lecture format and scaring him with her off-the-wall brand of philosophy. "Don't you have anything to say?" she finally asked.

"No."

Silence again.

Then, when they'd finished dinner, Cane placed his fork on his empty plate and filled her glass with the last of the wine. "I like your philosophy. But that only happens for some exceptional married couples. Not for the average, run-of-the-mill acquaintances, friends, colleagues."

"I disagree."

"And you love to." He grinned. "I get the feeling you've been looking for a great debate."

Her smile matched his. "That could be true."

"But we don't have that kind of relationship," he stated softly. "We don't know each other well enough to debate topics without hurting each other."

He was right, but his bluntness hurt just the same. She forced herself to keep her tone light. "That's true."

They sat in silence, with nothing but the soft lilt of music from the stereo to fill the void. Bernadette wished Cane was as ready for a relationship as she was. But it was obvious that he wasn't, and she was wise enough to know that. It wouldn't do any good to cry for something she knew wasn't there.

She wished a lot of things were otherwise, but had accepted Cane as he was before she'd asked him to move in.

"This won't work, Bette." Cane's voice sounded like a shout in the silence.

"Bernadette," she corrected automatically. Her gaze darted to his, immediately snared by his brown eyes. There was so much thought and feeling there, but it was as if he spoke in a different language—one she couldn't understand. "I beg your pardon? What do you mean?"

"This won't work. You're looking for something I'm not willing to give."

She rested her chin on her hand and stared at him. "Oh? And what would that be?"

"An in-depth relationship."

"Well, you've got me there. I expect certain rules to exist between roommates—all kinds of rules. And everyone who is involved in some way with others builds a relationship. But I didn't think respect and courtesy were some things that would be pushed aside."

"Is that what you expect?" He raised a dark, wicked brow. "Courtesy?"

She kept her expression bland. "Of course."

"That's all?"

Bernadette leaned back, never letting her focus waver. "What are you getting at, Cane? Are you thinking that I'm looking for a life mate?"

"Yes."

"Well," she stated calmly, "I am."

He covered his startled expression with a blank look. "Anyone we know?"

"No. I haven't found that special person yet." She smiled. "Have you?"

"No. But I'm not the marrying kind."

It was her turn to raise a disbelieving brow.

"Besides," he continued, "this business isn't good to marriage. There's too much traveling."

"My, that's a handy excuse."

"It's not an excuse, darlin'. But I probably can't convince you otherwise."

"You're right." Bernadette stood calmly, reaching for Cane's plate and placing it on top of hers.

"I'll clean," Cane said. But he didn't move a muscle.

"I'll do it. You cooked."

Cane just smiled. Bernadette knew she was being fair by cleaning, but she wished he'd protested just a little. It would make her feel better to know she was appreciated.

A minute or two later, Cane joined her in the kitchen and they worked silently side by side. Earlier frustration eased, then disappeared. By the time the task was complete, Bernadette felt relaxed again.

But Cane obviously didn't feel the same way. He disappeared into his room and when he came out, he was dressed for jogging in black shorts and a gray muscle shirt. He looked fantastic.

He waved in her direction. "See you later."

Then he was gone.

Bernadette stared at the news on TV without really seeing the program.

It certainly wasn't going to be a copy of her same old evening. . . .

Cane stepped out the gate of the apartment complex and jogged down Brand Boulevard. He didn't really want to leave Bernadette and jog; he just didn't know what else to do. He felt he was in over his head, but he didn't want to admit it to anyone, least of all himself.

But truth was truth. The lady was beyond him. She was more than he knew how to cope with and he wasn't sure what else he could do. To top it all off, he was torn to pieces.

He wanted her more than he'd ever wanted anything in his life. She made him feel wonderful about the world, his job, life. Himself.

He jogged across the Ventura Freeway bridge. So what had changed? He'd cooked a couple of meals for her, moved into a place that had a shower and a bed filled with the sweetest woman in the city. And his goal was still the same: He wanted to take her to bed and enjoy the experience.

The fact that he was caring more than he should was only a warning sign to keep their relationship light. Yeah, man. Keep it light!

Easier said than done.

The only thing he knew was that he didn't want to give up being with Bernadette—yet. . . .

So what in the hell was he doing outside when he could be inside with Bernadette? With that thought, he turned around and began jogging up Brand toward the apartment complex again. His jog turned into a trot. With luck he could be back home—not home but to the apartment—in ten minutes.

That was ten minutes longer than he wanted to wait....

BERNADETTE SAT on the patio, her feet propped on the balcony rail, wishing she cursed well. If she did, she'd be filling the air with a long string of blue words. But she couldn't think of more than two or three phrases, and they didn't seem worth the effort.

Instead, she scowled at the new planter holding her old plant. She'd placed it on the patio in the hopes that it wouldn't know the difference between here and its old spot, but it did. It was in shock from the move and transplant, but it would survive.

So would she.

"Now I'm gaining philosophy from a plant!" she said in disgust. But the thought was lost immediately when she heard the door slam.

Cane was back.

She smiled at the same plant she had just harassed. "See, I told you he'd be back soon," she murmured, plucking another yellow leaf from the base of the dreary-looking philodendron.

Cane stood at the patio door and smiled boyishly down at her. He wasn't even breathing hard. "Out here in the dark? Any reason?"

"None at all," she replied, trying not to let her heart trip.

"Well, darlin', why don't you come inside where we can both talk?"

"In a minute," she said, not wanting to appear too eager. After all, she hadn't come out and sat here to see if she could spot him jogging down the street, had she? Of course, she had, her conscience answered in its no-nonsense fashion. Damn her conscience. Couldn't it lie occasionally? Everybody else's seemed to do it. Why not hers?

"Can I pour you a glass of wine?" His gaze danced across her face, to her neck, then to her breasts. Her falcon's claw necklace fell between them, defining them even more.

"I'd love one," she said, remembering to swallow. Suddenly her mouth was very dry.

Cane pulled himself away from the doorjamb. "I'll get it."

He returned before she could catch her breath. He handed her a chilled glass, then lifted his own bottle of beer to his mouth and swallowed several gulps. She followed his lead, sipping the cool liquid. The crisp, clear wine wet her throat and she sighed. "Toad Hollow?" she asked. It was her favorite Chardonnay.

He nodded. "Tonight is a special occasion."

"A great-looking guy serving me a wonderful wine. What more could I ask for?"

"A bed that looks like it has just been used for a long, slow lovemaking session?" he prompted.

"By whom?"

Her answer was so quick, he laughed. It was a deep, throaty sound that she loved. "Us, preferably."

"Is that this night's goal?"

"It's been my goal since I first set eyes on you," he corrected. "And if my hearing hasn't gone, you said you were looking for a steady partner that you could trust. Right?"

She didn't want to answer that. She still wondered where she'd gotten the nerve to say so aloud. "And you're the partner?"

"Yes." His voice held an edge that tightened her stomach. "It's getting chilly. Are you ready to come inside?"

Finally, Bernadette swung her legs off the balcony and stood, stretching the tension out of her calves. It was the only place she didn't feel any tension.

With what she hoped was nonchalance, she strolled past him and into the living area, walking over to the couch and sitting down.

"You won't disappear while I shower, will you?"

Her laugh was light. "How can I? I live here, remember?"

"Good." He strode toward the hall, then turned. "Don't leave. You made the mistake of telling me your address, so now I know where you live, baby."

She was still chuckling as he jogged down the hall to his room. Anticipation sang through her veins as she wondered what would happen next. Would he come back and try to be sweet? Sexy? Noncommittal?

When she heard the shower running, she jumped up and ran into her own bathroom. She stared into the mirror and wondered what she could do that would drive Cane mad about her.

Her brown hair was sleek but plain, curling just under her chin. Her eyes had a touch of mascara, but no shadow. Her lips held a tint of lipstick, but most of it was gone.

Bernadette reached for her eye shadow but stopped just in time. If she put some on now, Cane would notice it and then he'd know just how much she wanted him to be attracted to her. That was the wrong approach.

The trick was to be cool, casual. Cane didn't want a woman who tripped over herself to get his attention. If her guess was right, he'd already had plenty of that. No, whatever was attracting him to her had nothing to do with eye shadow or lipstick.

She didn't know what it was, but she knew what it wasn't. It wasn't her great looks or wild and sexy ways.

The only thing she could do was run a wide-toothed comb through her hair and pray it was enough.

Just seconds after she returned and picked up her wine, Cane came into the living room. His wet hair was slicked back. His clean-shaven face was strong and forceful as ever, hiding the dimples she knew would pop out when he grinned. But it was his body that caught her attention. He was wearing only a royal blue towel that was tucked at his waist. A small patch on his shoulder still glistened with water.

He didn't stop when he reached her side. He took the wine from her hand and placed it on the table.

"What are you doing?" she asked, breathless anticipation lacing her voice.

"I'm taking you into your bedroom and putting you to bed."

"Now?"

"Now."

"But it's only nine o'clock!"

"Never too soon." He took her hand and led her to the bedroom.

When they reached the bed, he unbuttoned her sweater at the neck, then, with her cooperation, he lifted it up from her waist and peeled it over her head.

His breath whooshed in his throat as he stared down at her breasts held high by a cranberry-colored demi-bra. She didn't say a word, just stared at him with happiness that she pleased him.

With an expert flick of his fingers, her bra was loosened. Gently, as if she would break from the strain, he pulled the straps down over her shoulders, then let it fall to the floor.

"You're so damn beautiful."

"Thank you," she whispered in return. Placing her hand on his chest and feeling the hair tickle her palm, she said, "So are you."

Cane unzipped her shorts, undid the button and pulled both shorts and underwear down so she could step out of them.

Her whole body pulsed with his name: Cane, Cane, Cane. Heavy. Thudding. Wanting. "Unfair. One of us is clothed," she reminded him shakily.

"Not for long," he said huskily. With one thumb he loosened the tuck in his towel and it dropped to the floor as if by magic.

Bernadette stood stock-still. She couldn't have moved if she'd wanted to. In the soft glow of the bedroom lamp, Cane Mitchell was the most beautiful specimen of man she'd ever seen in her life.

And he was all hers.

# 7

CANE'S LARGE HAND brushed her shoulder, then grazed down to her breast until he held it in his palm.

"Your breasts are beautiful."

She answered him with a smile that showed how proud she was that she pleased him. "Thank you." Her hand stroked the side of his face lovingly.

Although reluctant to leave her, Cane took a step back. He flipped both the comforter and top sheet down to the bottom of the bed. "Lie down on your stomach."

"Oh, no," she began, backing off slightly. What the . . . ?

Wearing a smile just deep enough to show his dimples, he shook his head in reproof. "You've been uptight and stiff all day. I'll bet you have scrunched-up muscles you didn't even know you had. Since it's my fault you're in that shape, it's only fair I help erase it. I'm going to give you a massage."

She glanced down only to look up quickly again. Her face heated. He'd looked like he was more in the mood for lovemaking than a massage. "A massage?"

She must have sounded as stupid as she felt. His grin was knowing and sexy. "I'm giving you a special massage from head to toe, then I'm going to take advantage of your soft, slick body like you wouldn't believe."

"Oh, really?" she said.

"Oh, really," he repeated in a low, mocking tone. Gently taking her shoulders and turning them toward the bed, Cane steered her in the direction he wanted.

Bernadette took herself the rest of the way, stretching kitty-corner across the bedsheet.

"Put your arms at your sides and I'll be right back."

She raised her head. "Where are you going?"

The look he gave her heated her from the inside out. "To heat the oil. I don't want to chill you out at this stage of the game. Lie still and tell your muscles to rest."

As if she could do as she was told! Her body hummed with the thought of Cane touching her all over—even if it was under the guise of a massage. Her shoulders were already singed with the heat of his fingertips. What would she feel like when he had touched her everywhere?

One answer came to mind: liquid fire.

She felt his presence even before she heard him. Closing her eyes, she pretended she was relaxed, even when every muscle tensed even more, if that was possible. Small sounds seemed magnified in the still, warm air. A cap was flipped, there was a squirt, and then she heard Cane rub his hands together.

"Relax. I'm starting at your neck and shoulders and working my way down." He knelt on the bed, straddling her with his nakedness.

His hands touched her, warming her instantly. The faint scent of sandalwood filtered around them, adding to the luscious sensations. He eased her neck, then the back of her head, his callused fingers slick with warm oil. Cane seemed to know where the pressure points were, and went after them with the skill of a surgeon. After five minutes she didn't think she had a bone in her neck and shoulders.

He began working on her arm, then her palm, and finger joints on one side. Then the other.

She hadn't meant to voice a moan. It just slipped out in a moment of sheer, unadulterated ecstasy.

"I gather I'm doing okay?" His voice was low and sexy and had a tinge of satisfied laughter.

"You keep this up and I may put you on the payroll full-time."

"Wow, man. A real job," he drawled like a Valley guy. "What a concept!"

Her laughter was muffled by the sheet. But it was worth opening her eyes and glancing over her shoulder just to see the dimpled smile on his wonderful, full mouth. It was then that she noticed the fat white candle burning on the nightstand.

"Where did you get that?"

"It comes with the massage, ma'am. It gives just enough light to let me see what I'm doing without the harsh glare of a lightbulb."

Bernadette hadn't wanted to hear that. A small acorn of disappointment began to flourish in the pit of her stomach. "You're certainly prepared for everything. You're so prepared, you might as well go into business."

His hands didn't hesitate a minute. They continued stroking her thigh, kneading the muscle and teasing the flesh. He was coming awfully close to the apex of her thighs, but not close enough.

"I'm no virgin, Bernadette, but I haven't done this kind of thing before. However, I do keep candles in my locker all the time. I have to be prepared for blackouts. I go from disaster to disaster, remember? Just because I arrive doesn't mean the electricity stays on. I also have a gallon of water in my footlocker as well as a few other commonsense survival essentials."

She sighed heavily. "I jumped to conclusions."

He kneaded the other thigh, stroking and flexing the muscles. Again he came dangerously close to the apex of her thighs, but his fingers danced away. "Yes, you did."

"I apologize."

His finger traced a nerve on the back of her knee. Until that moment she hadn't realized how sensitive an area it was. "I accept."

But she had to ask the one question still left. "And the massage oil?"

He began on the calf. "It was a gift from another life. I'm not a virgin, remember?"

"Sorry."

"Don't be." He chuckled softly. "I never used it. Never wanted to. Besides, this is my big chance to learn how much I remember from football days."

"You played football?" His fingers continued to soothe as much as tone. Magic fingers, she thought hazily. Sexy, magic fingers.

"Only in high school."

"How come you didn't continue?"

"Because I didn't know anybody from my neighborhood who went to college. That was like visiting a foreign country—for people on the other side of the tracks. At the time, it was very important for me to carve out a niche in the place where I lived. For that, I had to be tough. College might have been a dream for other kids. It wasn't my reality."

"What a shame."

"You're not kidding. If I had made one choice differently, I might have turned out to be a person I can't imagine today."

His hand clasped her foot and began soothing her arch. It felt so good she wanted to make a satisfied noise again, but this time she kept her groans to herself.

"That's the same with all of us," she finally managed to say. "Each choice takes us on another path. Sometimes we can see the paths, sometimes we can't imagine them."

He stroked her ankle. "No. Some would be little changes. Mine would have been a big one—big enough to be inconceivable to me on so many levels, I wouldn't have known where to start."

"I'm glad you didn't. You're just fine the way you are."

Although Cane didn't say anything, she had the feeling he had an answer. That thought intrigued her. It was apparently something he didn't want to discuss, and ingrained politeness told her not to say the things that were on the tip of her tongue. But her curiosity didn't go away. If anything, his comments fed it.

When Cane finished one foot, he moved over to the other. Bernadette lay still, enjoying every nuance of every move. With hands that were strong and sure, he eased what little tightness there was left in her muscles.

Tension began building again, but this time it was of a different kind. Cane's hands, though still sensitive and capable, had slowed to such a languorous stroke that the whole mood between them changed. With slow, precise steps, Cane lowered her foot to the bed.

"Turn over." It was the most sensuous voice she'd ever heard, giving a command she couldn't help but obey.

With a lethargy she hadn't expected, invading her very bones, she rolled over and looked up at him. He still stood at her feet, his expression one of pure lust—so pure, it scared the heaven out of her. Instinctively she raised her hands to place them across her breasts.

"No," he said softly. His gravelly drawl raked over her nerves like wonderful, sun-heated sand. "You're so sexy I want to drink it in."

"Don't make fun of me," she pleaded. "I know what I am."

"And what is that?" he asked slowly, his gaze still drifting to various parts of her.

Without even thinking how it sounded, she began a litany of things she considered wrong. "I have heavy thighs, and stretch marks from carrying Ian. And my breasts are too small—"

Cane cut her off. "Enough of that. It's a bunch of hogwash. You're beautiful, sensuous and desirable because I can see your body and I know your giving spirit." He straddled her, leaning toward her face and planting a tender, sweet kiss on her brow and nose. "All I have to do is look at you and I'm on fire."

It was her turn to disagree. "No."

"Yes. All the rest is just plain crap."

Either Cane was one heck of an actor or he meant what he said. Bernadette wasn't fool enough to argue the point. Suddenly she felt she was everything he said: desirable, sexy, sensuous. Tears glazed her eyes. "Thank you."

Cane's smile was so deep, his cheeks dimpled twice. "You're welcome," he murmured.

Before she could respond to anything else he said, Cane had lowered his weight over her, dipping his head into the curve of her neck and leaving a trail of kisses from her shoulder to her throat. He then dropped his mouth down to one soft breast, whose nipple had already budded just for him.

She couldn't contain her satisfied groan any longer.

He touched and prodded and played with her; every movement was that of a gentle conqueror. And she loved it. When he entered her, she called out in instant release. His own growls of completion echoed distantly in her ears.

Their warm breaths mingled and their hearts beat so rapidly that they knocked on the other's ribs. Bernadette couldn't help the flight she took, holding on to Cane while she slipped off the edge of the earth. It had been completely out of her hands. Then, one heartbeat at a time, everything slowed down and they were sensually entwined on the bed again.

Cane slipped off her heated body to rest at her side. He pulled a pillow down and laid his head next to hers. "Don't move, darlin', and I'll get the blanket. It's time for a nap anyway."

Bernadette opened one eye and glanced at the clock at her bedside. "It's almost midnight."

"See? What did I tell you? It's time for sleep."

Bernadette pulled the covers from the foot of the bed up and over them. She placed a soft kiss on the side of his mouth, then one on his chest as she cuddled into him. "Good night, Cane."

"Good night, darlin'," he said, his voice already laden with sleep.

Bernadette smiled, then her eyes fluttered closed. Her last thought was that she was exactly where she wanted to be: with the man she loved. That thought was as natural as the deed—and as easy as breathing. Cane's arms tightened around her, but she was already as close to the source of her love as she could get....

WHEN SHE AWOKE the next morning, she was filled with the feeling of being all alone—not just in the bed or in the room, but in the whole apartment. She opened her eyes and stared at the stripes made by the light of morning as it seeped through the narrow-slatted mini-blinds covering the patio doors.

Cane was gone.

Her heart dropped in disappointment. Perhaps she was wrong. She'd been wrong before.... She slipped from the sheets and went to the bedroom door. "Cane?"

There was no answer.

She went into the kitchen and her heart sank as she spotted a note propped against the electric pot filled with freshly made coffee.

In neat, clean printing, he told her he'd gone to Newhall to check out some damaged houses and would be back sometime around five or six this evening. Meanwhile he'd left his portable phone number in case she needed him in an emergency. Otherwise, he would call her late this afternoon. If she wanted to work on the files, he had a few contents lists that needed to go into the computer. Then he gave detailed how-to instructions. His sign-off was distinctive. It merely said, "Stay beautiful," finished with a little hurricane weather symbol.

"You could have given me a small peck on the cheek, you whirlwind. It wouldn't have cost you anything and might have made me feel 'right nice,'" she muttered, slipping a bagel into the toaster oven.

After three cups of coffee and a bagel slathered with yogurt cheese, Bernadette got to work. Once started, everything went so well she thought she might be doing something wrong. She checked the instructions over and over, and finally felt satisfied. It was interesting to see what people had collected and displayed to make their houses their own special home. And it was just as sad to realize that all those items she was categorizing were gone forever because of Mother Nature's earthquake.

Later that afternoon, one of Cane's insureds called. Distraught, she spoke to Bernadette as if they'd known each other for years. Bernadette recognized the name—the woman was a prominent L.A. socialite who was mentioned frequently in the *Los Angeles Times* gossip columns. Obviously, disasters were great equalizers.

"And Saul gave me the twenty-eight Lladro statuettes—each for a special occasion. I can't believe they're gone. It's like the happy memory associated with each gift was smashed with them. I look at the blank glass shelves where they sat and my stomach turns over and I get angry all over again. Even though I know better, I can't seem to stop the feelings from overwhelming me."

Bernadette actually knew how she felt. It had happened to her, too. It didn't matter whether it was Lladro or jelly glasses, a David Hockney painting or framed posters: they all had irreplaceable sentimental value.

She tried to soothe the caller and when the woman had calmed down, Bernadette explained how she should itemize all her damaged goods.

When the phone rang again, Bernadette reached for it absently. "Conrad's Secretarial Service," she said.

"I thought this was Cane's answering service." Cane's deep voice was laced with laughter.

"If that's the case," she said, glancing at the clock and realizing it was almost three in the afternoon, "you're not very popular. There've only been two calls for you."

"Normally, I'd say that's wonderful luck, but I know better."

"Have you given this number out?" she asked.

"No, but it does go to a message center. By the time I get home, the center should have fifteen or twenty messages."

"Why don't you forward them to this number? At least there will be a live person answering. It usually eases the frustration level a little." She hesitated a second. "Of course, there is a small extra charge for that...."

"Sold at any price," he told her. "I'll turn it over now. Just tell everyone that I'll be back later this evening and I'll return their call then."

"Fine." Bernadette hesitated again, this time almost afraid to ask the question foremost in her mind. "Would you like some dinner when you return? I'm thinking of cooking."

"I'd love it. I'm gonna be dirty and hungry and need both a shower and food before I hit the computer."

"Fine. Take care," she said happily.

The phone was quiet for about fifteen minutes. Then it broke loose. Every fifteen minutes the phone rang and she had to answer a client's question or two. She responded to almost all of the questions in the same way: "I'm not sure, but I can have Mr. Mitchell call you as soon as he returns tonight."

Most of the callers wanted to speak to Cane right away. Bernadette figured they were used to speaking to him immediately and they were going to have to be trained to expect someone else on the end of the phone. But she found that the more professional she was, the more they responded in a like manner. Thank goodness! she thought, already exhausted after just two hours of handling Cane's clients.

At five she put on her own answering machine and began cooking dinner. She made fresh tuna with roasted potatoes and sautéed other vegetables with garlic toast.

Bernadette heard Cane's key in the lock just as she'd finished setting the table. Her heart skipped a beat.

Cane strode into the kitchen, looking at her through the bar, wearing a grin as big as California. "Hello, there, darlin'. How's the world treatin' you?"

"Just fine. It's your insureds who think the world owes them your hide."

He tore open the cardboard top of a twelve-pack of beer and began stocking the refrigerator shelf with the cans. "Well, isn't that just the way of it. They want my hide, but if they can't get mine, they'll probably settle for yours." His look became intimate and knowing. "Only they'd have to fight me for first place in line." With that, he popped the top of a can and walked through to where she stood.

She couldn't help the laughter that bubbled out of her.

Cane looked even more satisfied that he'd made her laugh. He sat down on the couch and leaned back, gave a tired sigh, then took a deep gulp of the beer from his can.

"Would you like a glass?" she asked, hinting.

"Nope. I like to drink this just the way it comes from the cow."

"The cow?"

Cane lifted the can and looked at it. "Sure. This is milk, isn't it?"

"Just like Mother used to make," she murmured dryly as she went back into the kitchen and reached for a glass of wine.

When she joined him on the couch, she told him about some of the calls that had come through. Cane explained the personalities behind the voices, sharing a few of their stories and backgrounds. Listening to his voice was just as relaxing as their sharing their day. They talked through the news and a sitcom before Bernadette realized they hadn't eaten dinner yet.

"Hungry?" she asked. "I'm sorry. I have it ready, I just forgot."

Cane stood and picked up his empty can. "No problem. Let me shower and I'll be right there." He sniffed. "Smells good. What is it?"

"One of my favorites. Hurry up and shower and I'll get it on the table."

Cane headed toward his bedroom and Bernadette began warming and serving the food.

It amazed her how wonderful it felt have him here. He was warm and funny, and quick and easy to talk to. Listening to him go on about the people he dealt with made her realize what a talent he had for putting others at ease. But that same talent helped him to keep others at bay. She'd bet that most of the time his insureds were so busy answering his questions that they never realized he hadn't given anything of himself in the conversation. He'd been safely hidden behind words that acted like an emotional wall instead of a bridge.

She recognized it. She just didn't like it.

She wanted Cane to care for her enough that he would drop his imaginary but no-less-solid wall. She wanted Cane to care enough that he would let her see the "real" man behind the bravado and humor that he used like a fence to keep her outside.

If there was anything she could do to bring that about, she'd do it.

When he entered the room again, he wore a black sweatshirt and a pair of matching pants. She knew what his body looked like under the loose-fitting clothing. Gorgeous.

It took her a moment to find her voice. "Coffee?" she finally managed.

"After dinner."

"Fine."

Cane's eyes widened considerably when he saw his plate. "This is wonderful. Fresh vegetables?"

"But of course."

He grinned as he took his seat. "As soon as this meal is over, please, marry me."

"But of course," she repeated, pretending a calm she didn't feel. She carefully placed her cloth napkin on her lap. But she was stunned at her own reaction to his jest. Her heart raced delightfully at the mere thought of being with Cane for the rest of her life. Her pulse beat quickly in her throat.

"Is that a lemon pudding I smell?" Cane asked, interrupting her thoughts.

"It's lemon pie."

His smile was smug as well as adorable. "I didn't think I'd ever fall in love. But you've created a miracle." He reached over, his strong, callused fingers wrapping gently around her wrist. "Forget waiting for the meal to be over. Marry me now and we'll eat later."

She had to clear her throat before she could answer. "Nope," she finally said. "I cooked this meal to be eaten in its prime, not when it's cold and congealed. You'll just have to wait till later."

The relaxed feeling between them continued throughout the meal. In fact, Bernadette couldn't believe they were so attuned to each other.

After dinner and dessert, Cane helped her clear up the dishes.

"You don't have to do that."

"Yes, I do. It's the law." With a determined gleam in his eye, he turned her around and aimed her toward the living room. "Come on," he said. "Sit down and relax while I finish up." He placed a kiss on her parted lips. "Revel in the idea that a manly man is doing the job usually reserved for the female of the species."

"What a good idea. Especially since I don't think the job has a sexual definition. I've always thought she or he who helps dirty, helps clean. You know—every adult does his share."

Cane went back into the kitchen and began stacking dishes in the dishwasher. "When I'm done with kitchen duty, ma'am, would you accompany me into the den and work for another hour or so?"

"I'd love to." She curled her legs under her and reached for the remote control. "But I'll wait for you to finish your chores before I step in there."

"Gee, thanks."

Cane poured the detergent into the dishwasher and shut and locked the door before turning it on.

Then he stood at the sink and stared over the bar at the woman curled into a neat little ball on the sofa. She seemed engrossed in the program, one long finger tapping against her front teeth. She looked sexy yet sweet.

Just looking at her made his body respond in ways he'd thought were for the more "studly" male youths. But it was more than sex that drew him to her—that, he could have anywhere anytime. No, this was an invisible connection that he felt so strongly, it sometimes consumed his thoughts.

"Hey, beautiful darlin', are you ready?" he called out.

She turned her head quickly, her dark hair catching the light as it swung delightfully—almost as delightfully as her smile that lit up and warmed his heart.

"Lead the way, human," she teased, unfolding her long legs and standing to stretch out the kinks.

He appreciated the view. Still, it didn't matter how he was responding to Bernadette, he wasn't getting engaged, marrying, or thinking about a longer-term relationship than the length of this "storm." He'd tried it once and it hadn't worked. No. He was single, would always be single. Marriage just wasn't an option for Cane Mitchell.

No. No. Definitely not.

There went that laughter again....

BERNADETTE COULDN'T wait for Cane to return home after a full day of scoping. She talked to him on the phone at least three or four times a day, discussing the latest calls, or files that needed to be pulled and notations made on their jackets. Occasionally, Bernadette made excuses to call just to hear his voice. If he couldn't answer, she got his recorder and could still hear him.

When Cane came home at night, they shared the kitchen duties, working together to make some wonderful, odd or spicy concoction for dinner. Bernadette tried to outdo Cane's cooking, and he relished the friendly competition.

It was fun and laughter and silly times. They shared, bickered, blessed, kissed and praised each other's work. He would serve her wine, she would open his beer. Every night he would seek the "sexiest" glass in the cabinet to hold her choice of wine, and she wasn't allowed to pour his brew into a glass at all. No matter how she cajoled, pleaded or questioned, he drank his beer straight from the bottle or can and refused to discuss it. Still, even that part of their relationship was fun.

She was falling deeply in love with Cane and she knew it. It was no flash-in-the pan thing that would die out after they parted. It was truly love. She just didn't know what to do about it.

Her instincts told her to announce her feelings to Cane and see what his reaction to a declaration of love would be, but caution warned her that he had to be brought along gradually.

Acting on the spur of the moment, she dialed Cassandra's number and left a message. Then she called Cane on his cellular phone. If she couldn't confront the man, maybe she could show him how easily she fitted into his world.

"Mr. Mitchell, I presume?" she teased when he answered.

"No, this is the president of the United States, but I'll accept a message for my good friend, Cane," he said without hesitation.

"Fine. Does he ever speak of me, Mr. President?"

"Well, little lady, now that you mention it, he does. He just said something about taking you on a scope with him tomorrow morning. He needs some help on a house where he has to inspect test pits. Think you can make it?"

"Certainly."

Cane's voice was low and intimate. "I know he'll be as pleased as a politician holding an award-winning baby for the camera."

"In that case, would you also tell him to come home soon because I've invited his friends over for dinner tonight?"

His tone changed. "Why?" The warmth and teasing were gone.

She hesitated for a moment, then decided she was wrong. There was nothing for Cane to be upset about. It was just an invitation. "Well, because I thought you might enjoy seeing your friends and I knew I'd like to get to know them better."

Cane didn't say anything and she became quiet, not sure what to say or how she had stepped out of bounds.

Finally he spoke. "Okay, fine. What time?"

He was curt, direct and to the point.

"I left a message for them to join us about seven tonight."

"All right."

"Cane?" She hesitated. "Are you upset with me?"

"No, of course not. Why?"

"Because you sound like it."

He sighed. "Do you always have to be so direct, Bernadette? I was just taken by surprise, that's all. I'm in the middle of a scope right now. I'll see you when I get back."

Bernadette hung up the phone slowly. Her brow furrowed. What had happened? What had gone wrong? All she'd done was invite his friends over for a meal. It wasn't that big a deal. They prepared one every night.

Another thing stuck out: "When I get *back*," not, "when I get *home*." He'd used such an impersonal tone, as well as a word that meant nothing.

It hurt. Were the teasing and warmth he usually showed her nothing more than an act? Was the underlying truth that he was only here because of crowded circumstances, not because he wanted to be?

If that was true, then he was only in her bed because she was available, and had clean sheets he didn't have to pull up from couch cushions every morning. It was not because he cared.

That thought did more than hurt—it was brutal.

But he had never said one way or the other how he felt about her. He'd never given a hint of his feelings other than taking pleasure in making love to her in the dark of night, enjoying her company, cooking and cleaning, appreciating working with her.

Could that be the extent of his feelings? He didn't care or love or need, but merely "enjoy" her?

"Lord, what have I done?" she murmured quietly. She had fallen in love with a man who didn't love her back.

"But he cares. I know he cares." Her answer was more a hope than a statement. It was also a prayer.

But she couldn't let herself think of that now. Besides, by the time Cane got home, his attitude might have changed. Perhaps he'd been startled by her inviting his friends. After all, she hadn't done so since he'd moved in, which had been almost two weeks ago. Nor had she even mentioned the idea before today.

Keeping that thought in mind, she continued to work, then began dinner early to eliminate any visiting problems. By the time Cane walked in the door, the table was set and the meal—a roast with potatoes, carrots and tomatoes—was cooked.

She was putting together a salad when he captured a beer from the refrigerator. His expression was curious. Casual. Distant. "Need any help?" he asked, bypassing the hellos.

"No, everything's under control. How about you? Need any help?" Bernadette gave a look that stretched from his head to his boots, then looked suggestively back into his eyes.

Big brown eyes that stared back at her blankly.

Her heart dropped down to her toes.

She turned to face him and wiped her hands on her apron. "All right, talk to me." She stared back at him. "Still mad?"

He took a large swallow of beer. "Never was."

"Oh, sure," she drawled, mimicking his tone.

Cane turned toward the hallway. "Stow it, Conrad. We can argue later. Right now I'm taking a shower."

He walked off, leaving a coolness in his wake that chilled Bernadette all the way to her heart. She couldn't understand his reason for it, but she knew it was real.

Half an hour later, Cass and Reed arrived. Bernadette greeted them, then led them into the living room. When they came in, Cane stepped out of his room, clean and sexy as hell. He ignored Bernadette, instead playing the jovial host with his friends.

"Hell, Reed, I didn't think I'd have to see your sorry smile for a long time." Cane reached out and clasped his friend's hand.

"You missed me, but you can't admit it. I know," Reed said, his grin as big as Cane's.

Cane gave Cassandra a hug. "Hello there, tiny mite. Good to see you're still surviving.

"Of course, I am. And now I don't have to worry about inciting you to a lusting frenzy when I walk out to get coffee in the morning wearing nothing but a holey T-shirt." Cass gave him a fierce hug back. "I miss that, you handsome lug." She turned and waved a hand in the direction of the kitchen. "Hi, Bette, how are things?"

"Cane must have been talking to you, Cass. It's Bernadette, and I'm fine. Both of you make yourself at home and let Cane wait on you," Bernadette called.

"Cassandra, I missed you. You always were outrageous." Cane laughed, referring to Cass's earlier comment.

"Like all the other women I've seen you with over the years, I always had a crush on you," Cass admitted,

sitting on the couch and staring up in mock hero worship.

A frown crossed his face. "Enough."

"What?" Reed raised his brows. "You don't want to
admit how you had to help Cass work through her
childish case of Cane worship?"

Bernadette fiddled with the silverware, unable to
keep from listening. Obviously Cane had convinced his
friends that his move-in with her was one of friendship
only. She doubted if his friends would be so open if they
thought Cane was having an affair with her.

"She was just a kid, for God's sake," Cane retorted.
He gave a forced smile. "And now she knows better,
don't you, darlin'?"

It hurt Bernadette to hear him call another girl darlin', but she knew it was a nickname for any woman
Cane knew well enough to tease.

"Yes, I do," she stated emphatically. "And I have
chosen to be your friend instead of your girl, because I
now realize that I'll be around a lot longer than any of
the women in your life."

"Amen," Reed chimed in.

"Cut it out, you two. I don't need a dissection of my
private life."

Bernadette turned just in time to see him cast a frown
in her direction.

"Oh, sure."

"Of course."

Both Reed and Cass changed the subject to the
earthquake statistics and their own insureds. Berna-

dette listened with half an ear as she got ready to serve dinner. She felt deflated and her spirits were crushed. Cane's friends' conversation had said it all. God, the truth hurt!

She was in love with a guy who didn't even want his best friends to know he was having an intimate relationship with her. He was willing to hide it, and was hoping she'd go along with it.

She wanted to cry. She wanted to howl. She wanted to scream. She wanted to kick the cabinets and hit the countertop. But she was a lady. That wasn't what a lady did. Instead, she needed to put a smile on her face and pretend nothing had happened, and certainly that none of this affected her.

Putting on oven mitts, she pulled the wide-brimmed dish from the oven and set it on top of the stove. Unable to think what she was doing for a moment, she stared down at it.

"Can I help?" Cassandra stood in the doorway, her gaze wide and open. But Bernadette saw just a hint of sorrow there.

"No, thanks. I'm managing fine." She placed the salad plates on the counter and began serving them.

"Listen, I think I might have stepped out of line a few minutes ago. I want to apologize. I didn't mean to pass myself off as a know-it-all. That isn't the case."

After a glance in Cane's direction, Bernadette concentrated on sprinkling pine nuts on top of the salad. Cane and Reed were deep in conversation. "I'm sure I don't know what you're talking about, so I wouldn't worry."

"I just realized that I opened my mouth about Cane's other women, and that's unfair."

Bernadette leaned against the counter, and looked the younger woman in the eye. "Are you telling me there wasn't any truth in what you said?"

Cassandra looked uncomfortable. "Well, no, I don't mean that. Well, maybe, yes."

"Then I don't think anything needs an explanation."

"I know, but I made it sound as if Cane has a girl in every city, and that's not what I meant to imply."

Bernadette's brows rose. "Cane doesn't date?"

"Sure, he does. Lots. It's just that . . ." Cassandra's voice dwindled off. Then she stood straight. "Cane has women falling all over him. But he's not some fickle, devil-may-care kind of guy. He doesn't get involved with everyone who makes an approach."

"I didn't approach him," Bernadette stated quietly.

"I know, but . . ."

"I understand what you're trying to say," Bernadette finally admitted softly, taking pity on the younger woman who plainly showed her dismay. "But I don't think Cane needs a champion. He's a big boy now and should be old enough to take care of himself. And his relationships." She smiled through her sadness. "And I'm a big girl, too. I think we know what we're doing. But if either of us gets hurt, it's between us." Bernadette prayed that wouldn't happen, but her gut instincts told her that heartbreak was exactly where she was headed.

"I've really botched this up, haven't I?" Cassandra moaned, her young face crestfallen. "I can't seem to keep my mouth closed enough or I don't say what I should when I need to...." She looked even more dejected. "This isn't my day. I botched it up with one of my insureds and now I'm doing an even better job with you. And I wanted us to be friends."

Bernadette couldn't help laughing. The young girl looked so depressed. As if the end of the earth were so easy to come to! She was still too young to know how cruel life could be and how much people could live through and still smile. Cassandra was so young she made Bernadette feel old. Very old.

"How old are you?" she finally asked.

"Twenty-six. Why?"

"Because I'm eleven years older than you and right now I feel old enough to be your mother," Bernadette said ruefully. How could she be sad when the whole situation was so funny? A young girl was trying to reassure her that a friend didn't fool around, when in fact he did. "Just don't call me Mom," she jested.

"Goodness, no one would ever know you're that old!" Cassandra exclaimed. "And you don't resemble my mom at all!"

"Thank you, Cassandra," Bernadette said dryly. "At my age we need all the confidence and compliments we can get."

Cane's head popped up from his conversation with Reed. "Is Bernadette giving you motherly advice?" he called.

"No, she's telling me she's not my mother." Cassandra's voice held a hint of self-derisive laughter.

"Hell, no. Anyone who sees her knows that can't be the case. She's young enough to be a mother of an infant."

"And old enough to know better," Bernadette added.

"Unlike Reed or Cane," Cassandra chimed in, then turned a dark red as she realized she'd put her foot in her mouth again.

"Are they wanting to be fathers?" Bernadette asked, looking at both men. Reed grinned but Cane looked frustrated with Cass.

"Don't all men want an image of themselves?" Reed laughed. "I'm not an exception. As soon as I find the perfect woman, I'm settling down and having a dozen or so little ones."

Bernadette found a lump in her throat and swallowed it away. She hadn't thought about those things in a very long time. A man in her life, a child on her knee—those were options her biological clock told her were fast approaching closed doors.

She shook off the thought and pasted a smile on her face. "You know what they say: 'Be careful if you find the perfect woman. She might turn you down because she's looking for the perfect man.'"

Reed flinched.

"Ouch." Cassandra laughed delightedly. "That's telling you, big brother."

"That can go both ways, little sister."

Cane watched the byplay between his friends in silence.

Bernadette smiled sweetly. "Sorry if I stepped on your toes."

"Truth doesn't need an apology," Cane declared.

By the time dinner was on the table, everyone had formed a truce. The truce was easy, Bernadette thought. All they had to do was stop talking and someone would fill the silent space with nonsense that made everyone laugh. Reed and Cane knew each other so well that they had a routine patter they fell back on. Routine or not, it worked to keep the laughter flowing faster than the wine.

Dishes disappeared by a miracle—at least to Bernadette. As if by unwritten agreement, everyone got up and carried their plates and silverware to the kitchen. While Cane turned on the water, rinsed the dishes and placed them in the dishwasher, Cass and Reed cleared the table.

When she protested, they overruled her.

"Hey, if we don't cook, the least we can do is clean." Reed's comment was delivered with a winning smile.

Cassandra's words hit more on the mark. "Cane insists on this routine, or he'll refuse to cook for us anymore." She laughed. "I don't know about you, but I'd rather eat his cooking than mine any day of the week."

Bernadette gave in. "I see," she drawled. "So this is a matter of survival."

"That's it," Cane replied. "I knew she'd catch on. You guys could have gone all day without explaining the routine. Until you opened your mouth, all I had to do was eat. Bernadette did the rest."

His friends hooted.

Bernadette relaxed her tensed muscles. Finally, Cane was acting like his usual self. Whatever had set off his bad mood was now gone. Relief felt wonderful, and she showed it by smiling at him as she served coffee and pie.

He returned the smile, but it didn't reach his eyes.

And the tension returned.

The rest of the evening was spent talking about the insureds and how to handle different code upgrades. They haggled about the differences between the last storm and this one, and then moved on to stories of other adjusters.

Eventually, Cass stood and stretched. "Well, you can marathon talk, but I've got to scope an apartment complex tomorrow, and I need all the sleep I can get."

Reed stood. "Yeah, me, too. Work comes too early in the morning. Thanks for a wonderful dinner, Bette. I've missed a good meal since Cane moved out."

"Face it, you missed me." Cane's words were edged with laughter. "I was the cement that kept you two going."

"Don't let it go to your head, friend," Reed said over his shoulder as he opened the front door. "We've managed so far without you."

"So you think you can manage another month or so until Bernadette's house is finished?"

Bernadette's heart sank. If this was his way of telling her he was leaving soon, it worked. She got the message loud and clear.

Obviously, Reed was as surprised as she was. His eyes widened. "Sure. Are you moving back with us, then?"

"You didn't expect me to—" Even Cane couldn't continue under the onslaught of Cass's and Bernadette's gaze. "Yes," he answered curtly.

Bernadette didn't feel the pain all at once. Instead, it slowly seeped into her every muscle and bone, building from a dull ache to a hurt so deep it felt as if it was knifing her soul. Her breath caught in her throat and she turned away.

She didn't remember doing anything. She smiled goodbye, and said something—she wasn't sure what— to each of them.

Then she walked into the living room, picking up the sugar and creamer, straightening the couch cushions and tidying up the room before doing the same nonessential routine in the kitchen.

Cane didn't speak. Instead, he got the coffee ready to perk in the morning.

Bernadette didn't know what to do. Should she ask him what was wrong? Should she ignore his comments until he was ready to speak? Not knowing what the problem was, was worse than knowing. But the closed, stormy look on Cane's face told her to back off and give him room.

She decided that retreating was the better part of valor, and went into the bathroom to get ready for bed. Perhaps in the middle of the night, when she was curled in his arms, he would disclose what was bothering him.

When she came out of the bathroom, the apartment was dark except for the light under Cane's bedroom door.

The pain in her heart got worse. He'd decided not to spend his night with her. That was as plain a message as he could deliver. She turned out her own light and slipped between the sheets. The bed was cold and empty. Tears slipped from between her closed lids and dampened her pillow.

Then, determination slid up her spine, making her stiffen with pride.

Instead of feeling lonely and abandoned, she was going to close her eyes and sleep like a baby. To hell with this helpless feeling. To hell with the awful loneliness. She'd been there before and had made it through. She would do it again.

She could take care of herself. She was sad now, but she would recover.

Bernadette brushed another tear away and repeated those thoughts a hundred times.

In his room, Cane paced like a caged animal. Which was exactly what he felt like.

It had started with his feeling of panic when she'd told him she wanted to invite his friends. It was that old responsibility of being an "us" again. He didn't want to be a "we" or an "us"—he didn't like the feeling. Just those words denoted a commitment that he hadn't yet made—one he hadn't been successful in so far in his life.

He was a lone wolf. He traveled life better alone than trying to drag a relationship along. Besides, whatever it was that made for a good relationship, he obviously didn't have it. If he did, he would have achieved it with some "lucky" woman already.

His panic had escalated throughout the day. Bernadette was mixing into his life in every area, and he didn't like that at all. How dare she load him up with this feeling of guilt at not being ready for this relationship! What nerve, that she should make him feel like a jackass for not wanting to present themselves as a couple.

Cane sat on the edge of the bed, his hands dangling between his legs.

How dare she make him ache with a needy depth of longing he hadn't known was possible! He both feared and craved what looked like unbelievable happiness with Bernadette; a relationship that would make him too vulnerable to find happiness and contentment by himself. But the biggest fear of all kept eating away at him: what if he gave it everything he had, and their relationship still didn't work? It would kill him. His image of himself would be ruined for good. He'd know then, with a certainty, that the dream of finding a woman and making it work with her would never happen. If it "didn't work" with Bernadette, it would never work.

Cane needed to pull back. He needed to be physically involved with Bernadette without getting involved emotionally. He needed to be with her without being a part of her.

Could he do that?

His conscience laughed at him even as he forced himself to say aloud, "Yes."

He made the decision. He'd make it clear that he'd be with Bernadette for as long as she was in the apartment. Then he would give her a pat on the back, a check in her pocket and let her go back to her own world. And, as long as she understood the rules, she'd be fine.

They would both be fine.

With a sigh that came from his gut, he leaned back, propping himself against the headboard. He flicked out the light, hoping slumber would come immediately and give him respite from his churning thoughts. Dim light from the apartment walkways lit the windows and outlined the bedroom furniture. Arms behind his head, Cane stared at the ceiling and waited for sleep.

An hour later he realized it wasn't coming. Instead, his wanting for Bernadette had grown so heavy and deep, it bruised his soul.

He turned away from the wall and purposely closed his eyes. The wanting turned to yearning. The yearning turned to need. He felt it build until he couldn't lie still any longer.

Cane stood and wondered what in God's great world would make this feeling of need go away.

He knew the answer; he just didn't want to say it aloud for fear of making it true. But his soul cried out the one word that acted like a salve.

Bernadette.

BERNADETTE TOSSED in her bed.

She wasn't afraid to admit how much she missed Cane in her bed—his warmth beside her, his heavy breathing, his reassuring pat on her waist or hip in the middle of the night.

She was afraid that her love for him would turn sour when he didn't return it. She didn't want that.

Another tear fell.

A light knock echoed through her bedroom. She stiffened. It came again. "Yes?" she finally called.

Cane opened the door and stood silhouetted in the dim kitchen light. He was bare-chested with a pair of black warm-ups hanging low on his hips. He looked handsome and dangerous.

Bernadette leaned on her elbows and stared at him.

Looking deceptively casual, Cane rested an arm against the doorjamb. "Did I wake you?"

"No."

"Bette . . ."

"Bernadette. My name is Bernadette. It may not be sweet or modern or short or cute, but it's my name...."

Cane came across the room and sat on the edge of the bed. His finger touched her lips. "Shhh. I understand.

It's just that it's such a mouthful," he said, a low touch of laughter in his voice. "But you're right. It's your name and I'll use it the way it's supposed to be used."

Bernadette relaxed. "Thank you."

He soothed her hair and the side of her face with a hand that shook slightly. "You're welcome."

"What do you need?" Bernadette finally remembered to ask.

"You." The answer popped out before he'd even thought it through. It was such a simple statement that it surprised her as much as it did him.

"Why?" She tilted her head and her hair shimmered with highlights. "You weren't talking to me all evening, but you expect me to be thrilled to make love to you."

Cane fought for the words necessary to let her know his feelings, but wasn't sure what his feelings were. He knew an explanation was needed; he just wasn't good with words about emotions.

But she wasn't going to cut him any slack. "Answer me. Tell me why."

"I'm not trying to jump in bed with you. I'm not that crass, Bernadette. But you upset me tonight because it sounded like you were trying to tie me into being a couple, and I was angry about it."

"Why?"

"Because you seemed to assume you had the right to do that, and we never discussed our relationship." His gaze was as strong and stern as hers was vulnerable.

"You don't want your friends to know we're living like a couple?"

"No."

"Is being with me something to be ashamed about?"

"No." He could see the sheen in her velvety hazel eyes and wished he hadn't come in here. He also realized her confusion, but it was nothing compared to his own messed-up thoughts.

"Then what?"

"Look, darlin'," he began, wiping an errant tear from her pale cheek. She didn't move. "You were the one who said we'd come together in joy, and when it was time to be over, it'd be over."

"And you're afraid I've changed the rules without telling you because I invited your friends to dinner?"

"Damn," he muttered. "I knew this was a bad idea. We should have just enjoyed each other without getting involved."

Bernadette tried to hide a catch in her throat but it wasn't disguised. "Damn," he muttered again, and pulled her into his arms, resting her head against his shoulder.

He wished he could cry and get rid of this rotten feeling. But he couldn't. That didn't mean he didn't feel the same pain she did.

They clung to each other in the darkness, needing to touch and be touched, to love someone and have someone love them, even if it was only for a little while. It was the age-old problem of being with someone and knowing that it wouldn't last forever. It never did.

But Cane didn't want to let go just because he knew it would soon be over. He wasn't ready for that yet.

Instead, he wanted all the love Bernadette could give him....

she concentrated instead on the near-destruction below. It would work its way up like wildfire, much like the dread in the pit of all her being, merciless, taunting. She

# 8

"WHEN DO YOU THINK my house will be ready to live in?" Bernadette asked, hoping she could keep a rein on her temper. The contractor had shown her every new phase of damage more times than she could count. The front part of the house was slab concrete and it was cracked all the way through to the back. The back half was on pier-and-beam, and was twisted and pinched. Because of it, some walls were being torn down to the studs, while another portion was being fitted with plywood to give added strength.

To Bernadette it looked as if it would be easier to demolish the house to the ground and begin afresh.

Stefan Allen, her contractor, looked down at his scribbled notes on a clipboard. "Maybe two or three weeks. A month," he added.

But Bernadette needed a more definitive answer. "What's the reason for the difference in time?"

The older man sighed and looked around. "The first two walls we opened up showed problems we didn't foresee. If every wall we look at has a problem we hadn't estimated for, we have to let your insurance adjuster know and see if he needs to scope the 'new' damage so he knows our cost increase is legitimate. Then we have to add that time and the extra repair work to the schedule."

"How long will it be before carpet and tile are done?" she asked, knowing that was the last step before move-in.

"Once the walls are in place, my crew will have everything else done in a week. This is the hard part. The rest fits together easily."

Bernadette brushed back her hair and stared up at the house. Without siding it looked like a skeleton rotting in the summer sun. "Will it ever be the way it was?" she murmured, more to herself than to the contractor.

"It'll be better. You'll see." He gave a harrumph. "I've seen worse than this and they come out fine. At least you've got good insurance, and upgrading the building codes is paid for. Some people are stuck building the same shabby house."

"I paid for the upgrade," she said dryly. "And it certainly wasn't cheap."

"No, but it's paid off for you. Believe me, you'll love it once it's finished."

But she didn't believe him. The home she and Nick had chosen was now a figment of her imagination. The place she'd loved so much was gone. This shell of a house was no longer a safe haven. She didn't trust that another earthquake wouldn't damage it, just like this one had. But it wasn't just the house she didn't trust; it was also the ground beneath her feet—and the ground around her.

Others seemed to have a philosophical view of things, declaring they'd rather ride out an earthquake than a hurricane. But she didn't think that she was in that category. The price was too high to pay.

Her peace of mind was shattered. Her trust was gone.

The contractor interrupted her thoughts. "We'll be repouring the slab tomorrow. By next week we'll be replacing the walls."

"Fine," Bernadette said tiredly. "Call me if you need me. Right now, I'm going back to the apartment." She gave an attempt at a smile. "You've worn me out just talking about the amount of work that still needs to be done."

"Don't worry, it'll be finished before you know it," he reassured, just before walking off to speak to one of the workmen.

Bernadette drove away with a heart that hadn't felt so heavy since her husband died.

Her home was destroyed. Her life partner had died, leaving her to fend for herself. Her son had grown up and left her to lead his own life, leaving a big gaping hole in hers. Her business was in ruins and she doubted she had the energy to begin again in a place she didn't trust. The only person she could trust was herself.

And Cane had been as distant this morning as he'd been last week when she'd had his friends over to dinner. He blew hot and cold, and that was driving her nuts. Sometimes she thought he was deliberately hurting her to see what it would take to make her run away.

What was the matter with her that she would allow Cane such power over her—that her emotions would go so crazy?

She'd thought love between two adults was more steady and thoughtful, and definitely less chaotic. She was thirty-eight years old, for heaven's sake. She should be more in control of her emotions than this! Instead, she felt as if she'd returned to the turbulent psychic state of an unstable teenager with zits and crushes!

The light turned red and she looked into the sunshield mirror just above her head. "Okay, Bernadette Conrad. Get your act together and pretend this doesn't hurt. Cane will be leaving soon. You might as well prepare yourself for it. Just because you love him doesn't mean he has to love you back."

She knew that, but it seemed strange to hear herself say it. It hit home more.

It was time to pull back and begin to retreat from this love she felt for Cane so she would be left with a little dignity when he walked out and she was alone again.

Although she knew better, there was still a small part of her that prayed that it would all work out; Cane would realize that he loved her and wanted to be with her for the rest of their lives, and she would be able to share the depth of her overwhelming love for him.

It was a fantasy and she knew it.

How silly could a woman be?

CANE WAS BACK AT the apartment and cooking by three that afternoon. He always thought better when he was among pots and pans and fresh vegetables. He was fixing rack of lamb with mint jelly and parsleyed potatoes.

He'd investigated several houses in the Woodland Hills area, then canceled the last two and gone to the grocery store for supplies. He had a problem to work out, and this was the best way to do it.

He wanted to run and hide somewhere he couldn't be found, to strike out at the first wall he saw, to yell at the top of his lungs. He wanted to do all those things at once, and do none of them. The truth hurt, and the truth was that he was in love with Bernadette. And that love was doomed.

He wasn't the right man for Bernadette.

He wasn't the right man for any woman.

He remembered saying that aloud once, and his friend Reed had laughed. "You're right, there, buddy. I can't imagine you changing one little bit to accommodate what's needed for a relationship. You enjoy your independence so much, I think you purposely throw those angry looks when you've decided you're not budging from your stance. It's enough to scare the bejesus out of me, and I'm your friend. I can imagine what it does to poor innocent women."

But it hadn't scared Bernadette. Instead, she'd looked back at him in calm question, silently wondering when and what he was going to tell her. In the beginning she'd been guarded, but since she trusted him, her guard was let down. Now, her face was as readable as a map he'd drawn himself. Her expressions carried every emotion she felt.

Accidentally, he'd hurt her several times, but never enough for her not to forgive him. He'd been lucky. He would get involved in something and forget to call and let her know he'd be late. Or he would go somewhere he hadn't realized that she wanted to go until he returned home and saw her disappointed look.

Yet, despite all that, he couldn't trust her to stay around and endure his uneven growth. "Please wait, darlin', while I do the growing up I should have done at a much younger age." Yeah, right.

*Trust.* That was the key word. If he put his trust in her and she violated it, he'd never recover from the pain. The alternative was killing him, too. Because he wasn't able to trust her, she wasn't getting what she needed.

He was hurting her and he couldn't stand her pain.

He remembered a book or a movie or something titled *I'm Dancing As Fast As I Can.* That was him. He was dancing his way around this relationship. It was wearing him down to a nubbin. He just didn't know what else to do.

THE NEXT TWO WEEKS were the strangest Bernadette had ever spent.

She and Cane worked hard together all day. It was business, and although they laughed and talked all day, there was a wall between them that couldn't have been more solid if it had been visible.

But the nights were different. She would climb into bed just after the news and read a few pages of whatever book had caught her interest.

This night was no exception. They had set a routine and it hardly varied. Cane closed down the rest of the apartment, then shed his clothes and climbed between the sheets, coming as close to her as he could without deliberately touching her.

Bernadette gave him a smile, then tried to read another few pages of her book. Cane flicked on the remote control of the TV.

A little while later, Cane watched the beginning of the Letterman show. His hand rested on her thigh or side or stroked her arm while his attention was on the television. When she turned out the light, he curled to the back of her, spoon-fashion, and kissed her shoulder—either good-night or hello.

All night long they held each other in a tender embrace. All night long they turned to each other, touched, sighed and stroked. If Cane turned over, he gave her shoulder a light kiss or caressed her side before moving. In each touch, move or sigh was a tender caring for the other. It was there plain as neon signs.

Bernadette had never felt such wonderful, euphoric peace sharing space and touch with another person. It was unlike anything she'd ever known.

Every day she wanted to cry with frustration at the daytime walls he built to shut her out. Every night she wanted to cry with sadness over his ability to show such tender and sensitive love within the confines of their bed only.

She needed to share her love with him. She needed to feel trusted and to trust him to be loyal to her as well as all the other emotions involved in that word. Neither of those needs were being met. And she had no idea what his needs were, so couldn't meet them.

It was a lose-lose proposition.

And, to top it all off, she wasn't feeling well.

Without telling Cane, she made an appointment for a checkup. Her stomach had been upset for the past three weeks and she wasn't sure if it was nerves or if she was cultivating an ulcer.

Once she was examined, she sat in the office and awaited the doctor's entrance.

Dr. Keiler came in, file in hand, with a wide grin on his face. "Well, tell me about the man in your life, Bernadette. Are you in love?"

She laughed nervously. "Yes, but I'm not sure about his feelings for me. Maybe that's what's causing this upset stomach." She looked at him, waiting for confirmation.

"You could say so." He glanced at her chart once more, then gave her a bushy-browed stare before sitting at his desk. "You're going to have a baby."

Bernadette went cold, then felt as if a wave of heat flowed over her. Her mind raced through the past few weeks and remembered the night they hadn't used protection. Just one night . . .

"Are you sure?"

His kind brown eyes crinkled in the corners. "Of course, I'm sure. Are you telling me it's not possible?"

"No, I . . ." She felt the heat of a blush add humiliation to her already unstable emotions.

But her doctor wasn't looking. He began scribbling on a prescription pad. "You look beautiful as usual, but your age might be a complicating factor, so we'll be keeping a close eye on this little one. You're going to take these vitamins and report to me in six weeks for a sonogram."

Bernadette covered her abdomen with her hand protectively. "When's the baby due?"

"This will be an early Christmas gift, somewhere around the fifteenth. You'll need to prepare now, though, because you're approaching forty. We don't want your system overtaxed by last-minute problems."

"Is everything all right?"

"Fine, as much as I can tell," the doctor reassured her. "But it's my job to worry for you, so please take care now so we can have a healthy baby later."

She walked out of the office in a cloud, jumbled thoughts tumbling one over the other. Her footsteps echoed in time with the words that repeated over and over again: *she was going to have a baby. She was going to have a baby.*

*She was going to have a baby!*

Despite the problems she saw ahead, she couldn't contain the happiness that welled inside her. She was going to have a baby—Cane's baby. No, she reminded herself with a jolt of reality. *Her* baby. Cane didn't want to be a permanent part of her life, and where she was, so was the baby.

For their child's sake, Cane would need to want to spend the rest of his life with the mother before he could have her support in being a part of the child's life.

If he couldn't accept and love her in his life, then he couldn't do that with their child, either.

As she drove into the underground parking, she made the decision to give them one more chance to successfully make it as a couple.

By the time she reached the apartment door, she was ready for confrontation. The only problem was that there was no one to confront. Cane wasn't there.

She punched the answering machine, hoping for a message that would tell her when he'd be home. Several insureds had called and Bernadette quickly wrote down the messages. The last message was for her.

Beep. "Ms. Conrad, this is your contractor, Stefan Allen. Good news. The foundation is solid and the plasterboard is all back up. We didn't find any other damage in the walls. The work has gone so well that we'll be done by early next week. Carpet and tile layers are coming Tuesday. Do I get a bonus for completing before deadline?"

He chuckled. "Anyway, call me if you have any questions. Otherwise, I'll see you on Monday at the site. There're just a few things I need answers on, and we'll be finished. Thanks."

The world was just full of good news, but she had no one to tell.

When Cane finally came in, Bernadette had worked up a megaton of nervousness.

"Hi." He gave her an odd look, as if seeking a reason for her expectant look.

It was time to take matters into her own hands. "Hi, big boy." She grinned, walking up to Cane. "Welcome home."

His brows rose in inquiry. Before he could respond to her gentle teasing, she cradled his head in her hands and kissed him full on the mouth. It was a long, tempestuous kiss, like the ones they used to have before either of them got caught up in the love ropes that seemed to cause them such problems.

Cane's hands came around her waist, almost spanning it. His low growl vibrated against her breasts, and she snuggled closer, feeling him grow against her stomach, where their baby rested.

Bernadette pulled away.

Cane nuzzled her neck, sprinkling kisses. "Please tell me whatever I did to deserve that. I want to make sure I do it again," he mumbled against her ear. His warm breath teased her neck and throat.

"You were kind to an old lady walking across the street," she answered, trying to keep her mind on her purpose.

"Definitely."

"You cooked dinner the other night."

"Of course."

"You made mad, passionate, exquisite love to me in the middle of the day."

He stopped nuzzling. "When?"

Bernadette pulled back and looked at him, eyes wide. "You didn't?"

Cane shook his head slowly. "Not me."

"Well, then," she said, a smile tugging at her mouth. "Don't you think you ought to take care of that little transgression right now?"

"Right now?" he echoed.

"This minute," she confirmed, taking his hand and leading him to the bedroom. "You've neglected me long enough. Besides, I don't want to be called a liar."

Cane looked bemused as she kissed him once more at the foot of the bed. Then, with aching slowness, she undressed for the second time that day. The first had been for the doctor, and this was for the man she loved.

With his gaze never leaving her, he slipped off his shoes, then undid his black jeans and let them drop to the floor.

Bernadette did the same, but her movements were as sensuous as she could make them. Praying she was looking as captivating as she felt, she continued in slow motion. *Please let him love me as much as I love him*, she prayed. The only answer she received was the look on his face. It spoke of a soul-deep hunger. It spurred her on. She was in a dangerous mood.

Believing this might be the last time she'd be with him to enjoy the freedom of having nothing and no one between them, she wanted so much to make this a memory they would both keep into old age.

Cane lay back on the bed, naked. He was so handsome, she wanted to cry. As he watched her with an intensity she'd never seen before, Bernadette continued her strip with languorous, rhythmic movements.

She smiled slowly and sweetly. "Are you still interested?"

"Stop now, darlin', and I'll yell rape to the whole neighborhood and ruin your reputation." His drawl was pronounced, his tone so low she knew it came from his gut.

She peeled off the last item and crawled onto the bed to lie beside him. Her heart was pounding so hard it felt as if it would jump free of her body.

"Wow, lady," Cane finally murmured as he enclosed her in his arms. His hands swept up and down her from hip to shoulder, his touch light and magical. "I'm stunned. What do you do for an encore?"

Bernadette gave a little laugh. "I haven't got the least idea. I was hoping you'd take it from here."

"Nope. You got this far on your own, you can go the rest of the way."

She looked up at him. There was a twinkle in his brown eyes, but there was still that hunger. It was the hunger that she needed to glean courage to continue. "I might goof. You might become impatient with me."

"You won't goof and I won't become impatient," he said softly, kissing the tip of her nose. "Any other excuses you can think of? If so, let's get them out of the way so you can proceed with what you're already doing so well."

Her tongue darted out and touched his small, erect nipple. His gasp told her she was on the right track. "In that case, let's see what I can do about taming a hurricane."

"Be my guest." His voice was as rough and gruff as her nerves were taut. "Please."

And she did....

Shadows disappeared and Bernadette was still in Cane's arms.

He was on his back, holding her close. Bernadette was on her side, a leg slung over his. His chin barely touched the top of her head. They'd been like this for at least half an hour, and neither of them was ready to end it.

"This feels so right," she finally managed.

"Isn't that the truth, darlin'."

She had to find the nerve to ask him the questions she needed answers to. "Cane?"

"Hmm?"

"Stefan Allen called today. He thinks the house will be ready to move into next week."

His hand halted in its stroking. "Carpet? Everything?"

"All will be done by Tuesday." She waited for him to say something, anything that might give her a clue to whether he was moving with her. Anything that meant she wouldn't have to ask directly.

Nothing.

"Cane?"

He began stroking her side again, but it was an automatic thing now, not the thoughtful touch of before. "Hmm?"

"What will you do when I move?"

"I haven't given it much thought. Probably move back in with Cass and Reed."

It wasn't the answer she wanted, but it gave her the courage to take a deep breath and say what was in her heart. "You can move in with me and we can finish the files together."

Cane pulled away, separating from her, and swung his feet over the side of the bed. She felt cold and bereft. "I don't think that would be a good idea."

She'd gone this far, she might as well go for broke. "Why?"

Cane reached for his sweat suit folded neatly on the chair. He slipped it on.

"Because you'll be setting up your business again, and I need some space to keep mine going. It will be better like this." He turned to face her, his expression as stern and unyielding as his words. She refused to be intimidated by it.

"We both knew this would happen," he continued. "You said you wanted it this way until it was time for you to go back to your world and I to go back to mine. Remember?"

"I love you, Cane." There it was, as bare as a newborn baby and twice as vulnerable.

His gaze softened, then he looked away. "Not really. In a few months you'll have all your boyfriends knocking down your door and I'll be lucky if I can get you to spare enough time for lunch."

His easy words fueled her anger. "Don't patronize me, Cane. I'm a thirty-eight-year-old woman who knows what I want and whom I love. I've loved before, and I know what it is." She stood and went to the closet. Still facing him, she pulled out a robe. With lithe grace, she put it on over her nakedness and continued, just as proud and direct as her actions had been when she seduced him earlier. "I love you. I'll always love you, whether you're with me or not. What you decide to do with my love is up to you."

"I can't do anything with it." It was a flat statement. It couldn't have been more definite.

"That's it?" she asked, keeping back the tears by allowing her frustration to show. "No, 'Gee, darlin', but I'm not the marrying kind'? No, 'Honey, if I thought I could remain faithful, I'd stay with you forever, but I can't be trusted'?"

He stood with hands low on his hips and stared back at her. His voice was so quiet, it shouted its message to her. "No excuses. Just no. I don't love you and I won't commit. I don't want a wife. I can't handle family life well. I'm not even sure I like children around. I might hurt your son's feelings, and that would really hurt you."

Her chin tilted. She would not cry. She would not cry! "I'm sorry," she said slowly. "I thought you might have changed your mind about commitment. Marriage. Family. I was wrong."

"Yes. You were. I had those dreams once, and I remember them well. And they're long gone."

Of all times, the earth began to rumble. The vibration began in the soles of her bare feet. Bernadette's eyes widened in fear. She reached for the doorway. Cane came directly behind her, one hand grabbing her waist while the other held to the doorjamb. The rumble built until they heard the building creak and groan from the strain.

Tears streamed down her cheeks, but she couldn't cry out her anger and fear. Her voice was paralyzed. *Not now!* her inner voice screamed, but no one heard. Finally, just as she was about to bolt for the door, the vibration got weaker, signaling the end of the aftershock.

Soon there was nothing vibrating but her own over-wrought nerves.

Cane's hands dropped from her waist and rested on his hips. He took a step back, then stopped. "I'm so sorry. I wouldn't hurt you for the world. You know that. But my work is my life."

Bernadette cleared her throat. "I understand that I put you in an awkward position. I didn't mean to." She took a slow, even breath, holding back the sobbing words she wanted to say. *It's just that I'm in an awkward spot, too, and I want and need your emotional support so I can give our child the best life I can. I need your love and care.*

"Bette," he began.

"Bernadette," she corrected. She held up her hand as if to stop him. "And, please don't make excuses at this late date. I should have respected your wishes and not delved into feelings I didn't really have a right to. I'm sorry. This whole messy scene is my fault and I should have known better. In fact, I think I did. I just hoped against hope that you had changed, that you felt the same way I did."

"You don't know me." Cane's remark stopped her on her way to the kitchen for a drink of water.

She looked over her shoulder. "I know. Isn't it sad? You know all about me, but I know nothing about you. That alone should have tipped me off that you didn't care enough. I'm sorry."

She left the bedroom and went into the kitchen and poured herself a glass of cold water. Perhaps it would cool the heat of her embarrassment for being so far off the mark about Cane's feelings.

A few minutes later, the front door closed with a loud click and Bernadette knew that Cane had left. He might have gone to Reed's or out to an all-night bar. Nothing underlined his lack of love for her as much as his leaving.

The glass hit the side of the sink and shattered. Her hands were shaking so badly she could hardly control it. Everything was hitting her at once.

When Nick had died she'd thought her world had stopped. And it had in many ways. But her love for Cane was different. This time she was starting out as a single parent, raising a child by herself without even the pretense of a relationship. She was alone as she had never been before.

Whatever happened—whatever she decided to do— it was her decision. She had to come up with a survival plan for her future. Cane was out of the picture now. She had to do what was best for her own emotional welfare and her baby's well-being.

She would not cry....

# 9

CANE SLEPT IN THE SPARE bedroom that night and the nights that followed. He didn't give an explanation and she didn't ask for one. Instead, they pretended that the arrangement was normal—the same one they'd had all along. Bernadette knew it was a case of major denial on her part, but she couldn't yet confront him and demand that he move out. Not yet, anyway.

They still worked together during the day, but it was as if Cane was closing all the files she was working on so he could get her and this work assignment over and done with.

Bernadette showed him what she'd done in other areas of the estimates. He was attentive and they joked just as much as they had before. But if there had been a brick wall between them before her declaration of love, now it was the size of the Great Wall of China. Every time Cane laughed or joked or complimented, opening up and relaxing for a moment, in seconds he would remember whatever it was that had made him decide to keep at a distance from her in the first place and he would close up.

Bernadette missed that easygoing part of him most of all. His new attitude made her realize just how much their idyllic time was over. For just a little while, she'd been given a glimpse of how wonderful having the right life partner could be. Then it was taken from her. She'd opened her mouth and lost it all—and she wasn't certain why.

The Great Debate continued in her head day and night. He had a right to know about his child, but she also knew it was easier, safer, to leave and no longer be a part of his life. It would only hurt more if they maintained some sort of contact and he found someone else to share his life with. She wasn't strong enough to put herself through that kind of emotional turmoil and still maintain a sense of dignity. It was better to leave and let both of them go on with their lives. No sense making life tougher than it already was. There wasn't even any sense in her trying to make peace between them.

Besides, it was too late to do anything about it. Clearly, from Cane's viewpoint, she couldn't disappear soon enough.

Making plans and setting them in motion was the only thing that made Bernadette feel in control. She'd decided she would be out of California by Wednesday.

Moving men came Tuesday and put everything in boxes. Bernadette and Ian organized and directed. The move into the apartment had been traumatic, but this move out was done with a mixture of regret and relief.

The night before the moving van arrived to take everything. Bernadette craved the comfort of Cane's arms just one more time. She wanted to feel him beside her, his body warming her once more before they went their separate ways . . . forever.

That night at dinner, she decided to speak out. "The movers will be here tomorrow."

"I gathered," Cane said, taking another bite of his salad. "All those filled boxes told me they had to return soon."

"Are you still moving back with Reed and Cassandra?"

"Yes."

She couldn't speak. She couldn't ask. She wouldn't ask.

But when night came and she turned out the lights and crawled into bed, she couldn't keep the loneliness at bay. When she heard Cane go to bed she ached with the feeling of wanting him close to her just one more time.

Finally, an idea came. Turnabout was fair play. Slipping from bed, she remained naked as she went down the dark hall to Cane's room. The light still glowed a gold color from under his door.

Taking a deep breath, Bernadette knocked on the door.

Cane opened the door almost instantly, startling her. She thought he'd call out and she'd have time to answer, to say something, to come up with an excuse for being there. Instead, he stood silhouetted in the doorway, wearing familiar black pants and exposing the same strong chest. He was gorgeous, and she was tongue-tied.

"Cane, I . . ." Her hand came up and brushed the invisible words away. She wanted to take a step back. To run. "I . . ."

Cane made the first move. He wrapped his arms around her waist and pulled her to him. "I know. Me, too."

Her hands stroked up his back, her sigh matching the movement. In his embrace, she felt as if she was finally where she should be.

He gave a heavy moan. "God, I needed to hold you just for a little while."

"Then why didn't you—"

"Too many questions. Not enough answers."

"Can we . . . ?"

"Not now," he said. "Maybe later, but not now."

And when his lips covered hers, Bernadette knew she didn't have any more answers than she'd had before, but she'd done the right thing by coming to him this one last time.

They were both thankful.

WEDNESDAY MORNING CAME too soon. Cane left the apartment before she woke up. He'd known it was her moving day, so she figured he didn't want to be around for any sad goodbyes. It hurt, but it might be best this way.

The moving truck came, put her belongings on board and drove off for her new home. She would meet it there in two days and find a home for her things in another week or so.

She wasn't going back to the house by the creek. The decision to leave the state had been made the moment she'd heard Cane's answer to her declaration of love.

There was nothing to hold her in California any longer. Her son was grown and happy in his own place. No matter where she lived, he would visit her. Although Ian was sweetly protective of her, he realized, perhaps with a little sigh of relief, that she was set on moving to Tucson, Arizona.

"Okay, Mrs. Conrad. Everything's gone except the clothing and personal items from that bedroom," the moving man said as he handed Bernadette a form-filled clipboard. "If you sign here, we'll be on our way. I understand you'll meet us in Tucson in two days."

"Yes," she said as she placed her signature on the form. "But the furniture won't be unloaded until the end of the week."

"No problem. So, you're moving out of earthquake country, huh?"

"I'm afraid so. But I don't think California will miss my little contribution to the tax base."

"Probably not, but I hope it don't happen too often. We need all the nice-looking ladies we can get," he teased. "Already got your place picked out?"

"The real-estate agent does. I've got two days to look over what's available and pick one so you can fill it up on schedule."

"Have a safe trip. Sorry you don't like us anymore. But out of all the natural disasters in the world, I'd rather make it through an earthquake than a hurricane. Went through one of those in Texas and it lasted forever."

"I'd take the Hurricane," she said with a lump in her throat, "but the Hurricane won't take me."

The head of the moving crew gave her an odd look, then left.

Ian came up from adding odds and ends to the stuff in his car and gave her a long, quiet hug, just like the ones they used to share when they lived together. Only now, he was a full head taller than she was and his arms felt more like a grown man's than a child's.

"Are you gonna be okay, Mom?" he asked gruffly.

Bernadette nodded, giving a kiss to his shaved cheek. Her little boy had turned into quite a handsome young man. Still, she wondered what her next child would look like. She wanted to tell Ian, but now wasn't the time. Later, she told herself, she'd ask him to spend the weekend in Tucson and tell him then....

"When are you leaving?"

"I'll probably drive to Phoenix tonight, honey. It's only three in the afternoon and Phoenix is six hours away."

Ian frowned. "You'll be driving on the highway at night."

She gave his hand a squeeze. "I've done it a thousand times before. If I get tired I'll pull into a motel."

Ian looked relieved. "And I'll see you in four weeks," he promised. "And you'll give me your phone number as soon as it's hooked up. Right?"

"Right." She gave him one more quick hug at the door. "I'll be fine. I promise."

"I know, but the world's not as pleasant a place as it was twelve years ago, Mom," he said with newfound wisdom. "There're a lot of weirdos out there. I wish you were staying here with Mr. Mitchell."

*So do I,* she wanted to say. But she wouldn't allow the words to form. Ian had taken to Cane the minute they met. He'd also assumed she and Cane were a long-term couple and hadn't wanted to think otherwise. Even after she'd told Ian she was leaving, he'd asked her to reconsider staying with Mr. Mitchell. She had carefully explained that their lives were taking different paths, but Ian was rooted to the idea that his mother needed a man in her life.

That wasn't to be.

"I'll be fine," she told her son.

Ian gave her one more hug and then was out the door, running down the hall to catch the elevator.

Bernadette closed the door slowly, leaning against it for a moment, her hand over her still-flat abdomen.

Another child. What a wonderful gift God had given her. She was as sad as she was excited, as tense as she was anticipating. And scared. Just plain scared.

Burying her emotions in action, Bernadette went from room to room, making sure everything was out of the closets and drawers.

Then she came to Cane's room.

Although the furniture was gone, his personal things were piled neatly along the wall, where he had emptied the drawers earlier this morning. The bathroom counter held his shaving items and toiletries.

Tears boiled up and she couldn't contain them anymore; they clouded her vision. She finally sank to the carpet and leaned against the wall, her head held in her hands. Tears turned to racking sobs that shook her body. She didn't know how long she cried like that. It could have been ten minutes or ten hours.

She'd loved and lost.

She told herself that, even though she'd lost, it was still worth the effort to go for the love she believed would last lifetimes. But it still hurt so badly, she could hardly catch her breath.

She wanted Cane to stride in and open his arms. She wanted him to say, "Darlin', I was so wrong. I love you and always will and we'll go through life together, happily ever after. You're too important and too wonderful for me to live without you."

"Bull," Bernadette finally muttered aloud to scare away her own fantasy. It had been Cane's favorite word in lieu of a curse word, and it worked. Fantasy wasn't the way life worked. She was woman enough to admit that everyone wanted a man on a white charger to rescue her, but she was realistic enough to know that that wasn't the solution. The solution was within herself.

She'd been alone and capable and competent for twelve years. She was proud of all her successes alone. But when a man—the man she loved—entered her life, suddenly she wanted to turn all soft and mushy and be dependent. Amazing.

And unfair.

Hoping she was doing the right thing, she told herself that this step was necessary. She wouldn't let all the doubts and fears of her actions claim her again. This was right, she told herself with more bravado than she felt.

She stood and brushed off her jeans as if she'd collected dusty thoughts.

"Cane Mitchell, you'll never know just what a wonderful chance you missed because you refused to look inside yourself and correct whatever image was wrong. You'll be alone all your life if you don't change. I'll grieve for both of us, but I'll be damned if I let all this sadness hold me down."

She walked determinedly into the kitchen and picked up her purse from the now empty bar. She needed to put a little backbone into her mental stance.

She grabbed a sheet of paper from the notepad in her purse. She deserved better treatment than Cane had given to her. She knew it. He knew it. Now was the perfect time to cut the cord and get on with life. This wasn't a time to daydream impossible dreams.

With a flourish, she wrote a quick note to Cane, propped it on his stacked clothing and left the apartment.

That part of her life was over.

She was starting a new phase now, and she would make a success of it. For her baby's sake. For her own sake.

CANE WALKED INTO THE apartment. The emptiness he'd known before was even more profound as he looked around. Everything that had Bernadette's impression on it was gone. He walked through all the rooms to make sure.

Ending up in the kitchen, he opened the fridge and stared down.

There was a six-pack of beer, an open bottle of wine, three pieces of wrapped cheese and one clean glass.

He reached for a beer, twisted off the cap and downed it. It was cold—almost as cold as his insides felt before he guzzled the liquid down.

"Damn her," he muttered into the empty apartment. Nobody heard.

He walked into the bedroom and sat down on the floor, leaning against the wall by his piled clothing. She seemed so close to him that he could smell the scent of her. He imagined Bernadette watching the men move her furniture out of this room. How did she feel, seeing his personal stuff piled against the wall? Did it faze her at all? Did she care that she was stepping out of his life?

Was she sad? Was she excited? Was she missing him half as much as he missed her? She'd said she loved him, but so had others, and they certainly hadn't meant it. The two women who had meant the most to him in his life—a girlfriend from his youth, and his wife—had cheated on him. Despite that, somehow, he knew that Bernadette wasn't that kind of woman. She was different. If she said she loved him, it was a fact. Then that should make her as miserable as he was.

He damn sure hoped so. He didn't like the feeling of being the only one who was lonesome. But the thought that she missed him as much as he missed her gave him solace. Childish as it was, he liked it. In fact, it was the only thing that took the edge off his restlessness.

Then he spied the note, sitting on top of his clothes. It was short, sweet and to the point.

I wish you all the best life has to offer. May you
find whatever it is you're seeking, and still want it
when you find it.

                                          All my love,
                                          Goodbye,
                                          Bernadette

He stood and crumpled the paper in his fist, wanting
to do something but he wasn't sure what. He couldn't
call Bernadette now and ask to come back. He wasn't
ready to humble himself yet. Maybe later, but certainly not now.

One look told him to move his things back to the
crowded apartment with Reed and Cassandra. He felt
for the ever-present cellular phone at his hip. Would she
call and ask him to come to her house? If she asked one
more time, he'd say yes.

*Damn. Quit kidding yourself, Mitchell. You damn
well goofed.*

He reached for his cell phone. He'd call and tell her
he'd come over. He wanted to feel her closeness, the
softness of her body. Her nearness. He needed to see her
hazel eyes light up with laughter and feel that sexy smile
light up his heart. He wanted to hold her close and not
say a word; just know that she wanted to be with him.

But he couldn't. Everything in him screamed fear.
Fear of commitment. Fear of failure. And that fear was
so overpowering he didn't think he'd ever overcome it.

Better to let it go now than to go through hell later
when he had to pull out and she was committed.

But instead of moving his belongings, Cane decided to spend one more night in the apartment before he went back to Reed and Cass's place.

A WEEK WENT BY and Bernadette never called. One long week . . .

Cane cussed and cursed. But he refused to call her. If she couldn't take the time to phone him, why should he bother? But as the week went into two, he became more desperate than angry. Why wasn't she calling—if for no other reason than to check on her final money? The next week came. The house had been completed three weeks ago and he knew that, aside from the money she was to receive on contents, she'd also made some corrections at the last moment. Between the two, she would have several thousand dollars left over.

He decided to check on her file. It took several days, but he got it back from the main office. Before he even left the catastrophe office, Cane flipped through the papers.

And when he checked on her payment, he found she'd made arrangements directly with the insurance company and had already been sent payment—in Tucson, Arizona.

His hand shook as he closed the file.

She'd moved and she hadn't told him.

He couldn't believe it.

With careful precision, he strode to his car and started the engine. He went directly to Bernadette's home. The concrete shingles shone brightly in the noonday sun. The newly landscaped lawn and garden perfectly accented the new paint and trim. And the sign that proclaimed it for sale was new, too.

Bernadette was gone. She had moved out of the apartment and she hadn't returned to her home. What hurt the most was that she hadn't told him what she was going to do. She'd disappeared from his life without giving him a chance to change his mind about their relationship.

*Grow up, Mitchell. She didn't owe you that chance and you never asked. In fact, you stopped any conversation that had to do with what was going on in this relationship. She tried to ask often enough. You just chose to ignore the problem—as usual.*

His fist hit the steering wheel. It was his fault. Not hers. It was time to place the blame where it deserved to be placed—squarely on his shoulders.

"Quit passing the buck," he stated through gritted teeth. "This was all your doing. No one else's."

By the time he reached the apartment, he knew he'd been handed on a silver platter the best thing he'd ever had in his life—and he'd shoved it aside as if it were worthless.

Stupid. He was forty years old and he'd never grown up enough to be an equal partner in a relationship.

Suddenly he felt overwhelmed by the weight of *all* the mistakes he'd made in *all* his relationships.

He could be charming enough to bring everyone laughter and fun. But he couldn't sustain it. It was an act—a part of him that wasn't real. Even as he told jokes, he knew he was using his wit as a method of guarding himself against anyone coming any closer to him.

Especially the woman he loved.

He'd gotten scared of love and so he'd pulled away from her, first. He couldn't control the situation, so he'd opted out of it.

Cane pulled into the underground garage and sat in the dark truck. He closed his eyes and leaned his head back, knowing he had to think this through before seeing his friends. They would distract him. Besides, he didn't know what to say to them. Better to stay here until he absorbed it all. He had some heavy thinking to do, and this was only the beginning. He could continue to do what he'd done all his life—run and hide— or he could face it. But he had to make one decision or the other. Now was the time to come to terms with his life.

He'd always blamed someone else for his problems. He'd always passed the buck; the way he was raised, his worthless education, the wrong side of the tracks—all had made him make decisions that were wrong. He'd always gone for the wrong woman, so therefore there weren't any right women. They were all liars and cheats.

He used every excuse in the book. Some he believed and some he didn't, but it didn't matter as long as he kept the blame from falling on himself. As long as he didn't accept the blame, he had his pride.

But his pride bred loneliness. There was no one to blame for that except himself.

Part of him needed love so much, he withered from lack of it. At the same time, part of him was so afraid that it made sure he couldn't have access to it.

He was a torn man.

A tear squeezed out from his eyelids. Another one followed. Then came the sobs. He cried like he hadn't cried since he was five years old and his mother had finally left for good. He cried away some of the anger and the hate that he'd bred and held inside. He cried for lost chances and broken promises. He cried for lost love. The lost love of Bernadette.

THANKS TO A SAVVY real-estate agent, Bernadette found her new home within hours of arriving in Tucson. It was in the foothills of the mountains that surrounded the city. The house had three bedrooms, a den large enough to be her office, and a view of the city lights from almost every room. A covered patio ran the length of the whole house, shading the sliding-glass doors and windows facing out. Her room—the master bedroom—was the highlight. One wall was floor-to-ceiling glass, one mirrored to reflect the exterior, and one was adobe brick. The room was so different from what she was used to, and yet she loved it.

The best part was that the new house was affordable. She had enough money to hold the option price and the out-of-state owners said she could pay the balance when she sold her own home in California. Two days after finding it, she had her belongings moved in. Two days after that, she was set up with a doctor. And a week later, she had cards printed and was ready to begin a secretarial business. But first, she decided to do some work for a temporary service so she could learn more about the city and its business community.

She took a monthlong job with an attorney's firm. It was tough work but it was better to do it now than wait until her pregnancy began to show. By that time, she wanted to be established enough to have clients who depended upon her. She wasn't going to spend a dime out of the way right now. Although she had money for the time being, things could get tough down the road.

By the end of the week, she was satisfied she'd made the right choice in moving. She loved the desert, but she also loved the lack of rocking earth under her feet. Here she would deal with floods of rain, occasional snow and hotter weather than Los Angeles had ever dreamed about. But she'd found her niche—at least for now.

And as much as she was happy with her new home, she was also excited and awed by her pregnancy. There weren't too many moments when she didn't think of the baby she was carrying—or the baby's father.

She should have been unhappy about this pregnancy, but she wasn't. It didn't matter that she was an older woman unmarried and pregnant, that she had no visible means of support right now, or that she had no prospects of help in raising this child.

What mattered was that she was going to be a mother again—she would have someone in this life to love—and that she had loved the child's father with all her heart. It hadn't been a planned pregnancy, but it was certainly a wanted one.

It would have been wonderful if—

No ifs! she told herself. This was the way things were, and she had to work with what she had.

But the natural mood swings that came with pregnancy also gave her room to pause and wonder why Cane would shut out her love so completely. Try as she might, she never came up with an answer.

She woke up early every morning, gagged down saltines, and dressed for work. She was out of the driveway by seven-thirty and at work by eight. If she still lived in L.A., she'd be in traffic for over double that time.

By the time Bernadette was into her third week of the job, however, she was exhausted. Everything had happened so quickly and she'd had so much to do that she'd never had a chance to rest between challenges.

In the evenings, she dragged home and rested for an hour or so before fixing something to eat and getting ready for the next day. It was a ritual, but one that the baby reminded her was important.

She missed the few girlfriends she'd had in California, but surprisingly, they had moved on in their careers, too. Her best friend, Talia, had moved to Santa Fe just weeks before the earthquake, but promised she'd come visit soon.

She'd made new friends with a few of the women in the law office where she worked, and with the real-estate agent who'd found her house. They would occasionally drop by and have a glass of wine or join her in a soft drink, but that was the extent of her entertainment schedule.

It gave her lots of time to think of Cane. Too much time . . .

CANE GLANCED DOWN at the sheet of crumpled paper with Bernadette's address scribbled on it once more, then at the mailbox beside the steep driveway. It was the same. He turned into the driveway and drove up under the olive tree, leaving the carport empty.

This was Bernadette's house.

Her car wasn't here, but he knocked on the door anyway. There was no answer.

His boots crunched on the gravel as he walked around the side of the house and looked for an open gate to enter the sloping yard. There was none. Instead, he stepped back, and with a jump, vaulted the lowest side of the adobe fence.

Her backyard had grass on one half—an unusual commodity in Tucson. The other half held a pool surrounded by fruit trees and berry bushes. Scattered everywhere were large colorful pots filled with lush, fat cacti. Sloping eaves ran the length of the back of the house, acting as a cover for the patio. In the shade, Bernadette had arranged a round table and four chairs, and two long, comfortable lounge chairs, all upholstered in forest green with gray stripes. It looked like Bernadette—cozy, comfortable, and very classy.

Cane walked the perimeter of the fenced yard. From the outside the house was a dollhouse. He shaded his eyes and looked in the windows, knowing beforehand that he'd like what he saw. Although this place was a little smaller than her house in California, her furniture seemed to blend beautifully with the Southwestern decor.

A glance at his watch told him it was a little after four in the afternoon. He'd left Glendale around six this morning and had gotten caught in every traffic jam in every town.

Deciding he might as well make himself comfortable, Cane stretched out on the lounge chair, wishing he was inside her bedroom instead of just outside of it. Maybe, with a lot of luck and prayer, and some honest discussion, he could be with her tonight.

Everybody had to have hope. He just wasn't sure if Bernadette had any left for this relationship.

WHEN BERNADETTE DROVE up the drive, she was exhausted. It was the end of the third week of this job, and she hoped that the weekend would refresh her enough to be able to hang on for one more week.

But when she saw the black GMC truck under her olive tree, her heartbeat quickened its pace as if she'd run a ten-mile race.

Okay, she told herself. So Cane was here. Big deal.

Maybe it had something to do with her insurance claim.

Maybe it had something to do with the work she'd done for him.

Maybe she was kidding herself.

She parked the car and walked directly into the house and closed the door behind her. Cool air soothed her heated skin. Pretending she wasn't worried about where he was, she kept to her usual routine.

Dropping her purse on the couch, Bernadette went straight to the kitchen and made herself a cup of tea. After adding several spoonfuls of honey, she walked into her bedroom. Through the gauzy drapes she saw his form on the chaise longue. He was shielded from the sun by the orange tree. His booted feet were crossed, his hands dangling from the arms of the chair. He certainly was relaxed for being in someone else's territory.

With one eye on him, she changed out of work clothes and switched into a loose-fitting shorts set. Then she walked around the house, straightening up the kitchen, putting away her purse.

But every nerve in her body cried out in curiosity. How could she talk to him and find out what he wanted without letting him know she was carrying their child? She didn't think she could stand it if he gave her one of those keep-your-distance looks.

For the sake of the baby, she had to carry this confrontation off and get rid of him.

Opening the dining-room glass doors, she went out and stood at the foot of the chaise longue.

"Cane?" she called a little louder than necessary. "What are you doing here?"

Cane opened his eyes and squinted into the sun, his gaze focusing slowly. Then came his smile and just the beginning of it melted her heart to the consistency of jelly. "Hello, darlin'. My, you are a beautiful sight. I missed you so much."

"What are you doing here?"

Cane prepared to stand, swinging his long legs over the side of the lounge. "I plan on holding you in my arms and telling you how wrong I was."

Bernadette took a step back. "I'm not going into your arms but I accept your apology. Now, please leave."

"Bernadette," he said, his smile gone. "Please, let's talk a little. I have a lot to explain. Don't close the door on me."

"Go away."

Bernadette took a few more steps back. "There's nothing else to say. Goodbye." And she quickly slipped inside, closing the sliding door behind her and placing the wooden rod in the track so it couldn't be opened.

Her hands shook, her breath was so erratic she could barely catch it. She walked directly into the kitchen and splashed her face with cool water. He had to go back to Glendale. He just had to!

It was as if he'd read her thoughts. He spoke through the glass door. "I'm not going until I have a chance to explain. Darlin', I love you and I'm not leaving until you hear me out."

She turned to face him through the sliding-glass door, staring him down. Then, with a quiet, cold feeling in the pit of her stomach, Bernadette marched over to the door and pulled the insulated curtain closed.

He might love her right now, but he was a fickle man. Throughout their relationship he'd run hot and cold without giving reasons for it. Besides, when he learned that she had hidden from him the one thing he wanted, he would hate her. She couldn't take that. She couldn't take the thought of sharing the baby with a man who hated her.

With methodical movements, Bernadette fixed herself a bowl of soup for dinner. The baby had to eat, even if she didn't feel like it. Afterward, she cleaned up.

Cane was still outside in the backyard. Occasionally, he called to her to open the door, but she refused to acknowledge his presence.

Bernadette was relieved to see the clock turn to ten. It was time for bed. She set about closing the house for the night. With every step, she prayed that Cane would go back to California. Go away. Disappear. Let her alone.

She changed into her long nightgown and turned out the light. A bright orange full moon outlined Cane against her window. He stood no more than two feet from the side of her bed. A rod in the track allowed the door to be opened no more than an inch or so for fresh air without allowing access.

"You look beautiful, Bernadette," he said. His voice was all soft and thick, just the way he used to talk when they were holding each other in bed at night. "I was a stupid fool to throw it all away."

She scooted to the other side of the bed as if distance would help keep him at bay.

"I was wrong, Bernadette. I'm sorry."

"Yes, you were."

"I want a second chance."

"That's nice."

"Give me one, Bernadette. Give us both a chance. Please."

Leaning up on her elbows, she stared at him through the gauzy curtains. "Why?"

"Because I love you. We belong together. I'll prove it to you."

"Nobody belongs together unless it's good for both of them. You showed me it wasn't good for me. In fact, you made sure I understood that."

"I said I was wrong!"

"Congratulations. But it just doesn't seem fair to take you at your word, since you give and take away so easily."

She lay down and turned over, curling into herself as she tried to keep her back to him. Tears started to flow when she heard his bootsteps echo down the patio walk toward the gate. He was going. Her secret was safe.

And her pride was in tatters. She'd gone to him that last night and let him see how much she needed to be in his arms. But when he rejected her, he'd shattered her faith and trust. No one could live without faith and trust in the person they loved.

The bootsteps came back. Bernadette stiffened, waiting for the next onslaught to her senses. The lounge chair scraped against concrete.

"I'm staying, darlin'," he finally stated. "I love you and I'm not going back to California until you admit you love me, too. We both know it's true. Besides, I need you in my life to help me find my joy, Bernadette Conrad. I love you more than I need air to breathe."

"You didn't take care of my love when you had it," she countered through the closed glass door.

"That's what life's lessons are about, honey. I need a second chance to prove that I learned my lesson. I need that second chance to show you how happy we can be together. I promise I'll never ask for a third chance, because I'll never need it."

Bernadette gave a disbelieving harrumph. Then she peeped over her shoulder.

Cane spread his blanket over his legs and she knew that the chilled desert air would penetrate his clothing soon. "Sleep well, my love," he drawled to the glass door.

She uncurled and stared through the door. She wanted this baby above all else, but if someone asked what her next want was, it would be that Cane would want her in his life as much she wanted him to be there. If she was chasing him out because of her secret, wasn't she doing the same thing he'd done? She suspected he'd chased her out because he was afraid she would go sooner or later.

She was guilty of the same action.

*Take a chance,* the little voice inside her said. And she knew it was right. If she didn't take that chance just one more time, she knew she'd be alone all her life. No one but Cane would do.

She tossed and turned with all her thoughts and alternatives. Fifteen minutes later, a resigned Bernadette slid open the door and stared down at him.

Cane gave a dimpled smile despite the fact that he looked like an icy Popsicle.

"Will you work on your lone-wolf attitude?"

"Yes."

"Will you go to counseling to learn to deal with intimacy?" she demanded.

She gave him credit. He hesitated only a minute before nodding. "Yes."

"Are you interested in marriage and children?"

"Yes. Always was. I just didn't want to say so. Everything I ever wanted and said aloud, I never got. It got to be a superstition."

She gave him a disbelieving look, but she didn't walk away. "Are you going to panic and try to shoot this relationship in the foot anymore?"

Cane stood and faced her, letting the blanket drop to the concrete. His expression was heartbreakingly filled with love. "No. I know what I want, and it's right here in front of me. Forever."

Bernadette knew when to give in. She also knew she couldn't tell him anything now. Later. Tomorrow. The baby wouldn't mind waiting another day to be formally introduced to its father. She sighed. "Come to bed and we'll talk about it in the morning." She reached for his hand and turned. But when she took a step inside the bedroom, he remained rooted where he was.

She looked back, surprised.

"Will you give me some time to learn how to be a couple?" he asked.

"Yes," she whispered, realizing just how vulnerable he felt. She'd thought she was the only one....

"And will you allow me to make a mistake occasionally until I learn how to be the kind of partner you need?"

"As long as they're little mistakes."

"And do you want a formal wedding or can we elope?"

Her solemn expression turned into a broad grin. "A formal wedding. A big one."

"Damn," he muttered. "I had a feeling you'd say that."

"Then you shouldn't have asked."

"Well, darlin', I'm not in favor of big weddings but if it's what pleases you, I'll sacrifice myself on the altar of love." His voice held a resigned sigh.

"Is that all?" she asked, a smile tilting the corners of her mouth.

"One more thing. How committed are you to living in Tucson? I've got my eye on this piece of land...."

She realized what he was saying. He'd dreamed of being a rancher in his own home state of Texas. While she ... "As long as I'm with you, I can live anywhere except California. Here, Texas, wherever. It's all the same as long as you're there, my Hurricane."

"Oh, Bernadette, you do know how to sing to me sweetly," he said in a low, deep voice.

Holding out her hand, she pulled him closer. When his arms encircled her waist, she whispered in his ear. "And now come to bed. I've got so much to do tomorrow. After all," she teased, "I've got a wedding to plan and I still have to make it as painless as possible for you."

"Good."

"Besides, I don't have that many people to invite." Bernadette stepped back into the room and Cane followed, closing the sliding door behind him.

"What about children?" she asked. Reaching for his shirt buttons, she undid them one by one.

"I want a dozen."

Bernadette's hands fumbled. "A dozen? I thought you were kidding and didn't really want any."

"I lied." His hands covered hers. "But if you don't want any, that's okay, too. I want you more than I've ever wanted anything in my life. I need your love just to be at peace, Bette. The rest is just window dressing."

Taking a deep breath, she moved his hands down to her abdomen, cradling the slight roundness there. "Hurricane Mitchell, if you run from me now, know that you'll be running from two of us. There will be no third chance for either one. We either commit to be together and raise this child with all the love and caring we all deserve, or we call it off now, while I can still function without you."

His eyes were filled with wonder. "My child?"

She nodded.

"Our child."

She nodded again.

Cane closed his eyes and heaved a great sigh. "Dear God, I never thought this day would actually happen."

She stroked the side of his face. "What day?"

He opened his eyes and stared down at her as if he wanted to devour her alive. "The day that I would be holding the only woman I ever loved and she would be carrying my baby."

"It's true, it's really true." She smiled. "And if we're not with you, you'll hold us every time you return from chasing storms from one end of the coast to the other."

She kissed the tip of his chin, thanking her stars for finding the nerve to open that door and invite him in. A shiver ran down her spine at the thought of letting all this happiness go because of her silly pride. . . .

"First things first. It's late and you should be in bed." His hands ran up and down her arms, warming her. But he looked doubtful. "Are you sure?"

"Positive." Her smile told him how certain she was.

It was his turn to smile, melting her heart with the tenderness of it. "Yes, ma'am," he said in his best Texas drawl. "We've got to start practicing to be good parents."

"First we have to be good to each other," she corrected softly. "Here, I'll show you how."

And she did. . . .

Women throughout time have
lost their hearts to:

Starting in January 1996, Harlequin Temptation
will introduce you to five irresistible, sexy rogues.
Rogues who have carved out their place in history,
but whose true destinies lie in the arms of
contemporary women.

#569 *The Cowboy*, Kristine Rolofson
(January 1996)

#577 *The Pirate*, Kate Hoffmann
(March 1996)

#585 *The Outlaw*, JoAnn Ross
(May 1996)

#593 *The Knight*, Sandy Steen
(July 1996)

#601 *The Highwayman*, Madeline Harper
(September 1996)

Dangerous to love, impossible to resist!

## MILLION DOLLAR SWEEPSTAKES

SWP-H296

BRIDE'S
BAY RESORT

## UNLOCK THE DOOR TO GREAT ROMANCE AT BRIDE'S BAY RESORT

Join Harlequin's new across-the-lines series, set in an exclusive hotel on an island off the coast of South Carolina.

Seven of your favorite authors will bring you exciting stories about fascinating heroes and heroines discovering love at Bride's Bay Resort.

Look for these fabulous stories coming to a store near you beginning in January 1996.

**Harlequin American Romance #613** in January
*Matchmaking Baby* by Cathy Gillen Thacker

**Harlequin Presents #1794** in February
*Indiscretions* by Robyn Donald

**Harlequin Intrigue #362** in March
*Love and Lies* by Dawn Stewardson

**Harlequin Romance #3404** in April
*Make Believe Engagement* by Day Leclaire

**Harlequin Temptation #588** in May
*Stranger in the Night* by Roseanne Williams

**Harlequin Superromance #695** in June
*Married to a Stranger* by Connie Bennett

**Harlequin Historicals #324** in July
*Dulcie's Gift* by Ruth Langan

Visit Bride's Bay Resort each month wherever
Harlequin books are sold.

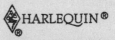

HARLEQUIN®

BBAYG

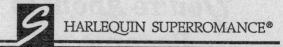

# HARLEQUIN SUPERROMANCE®

From the bestselling author of
**THE TAGGARTS OF TEXAS!**
comes

## Cupid, Colorado...

This is ranch country, cowboy country—a land of high mountains and swift, cold rivers, of deer, elk and bear. The land is important here—family and neighbors are, too. 'Course, you have the chance to really get to know your neighbors in Cupid. Take the Camerons, for instance. The first Cameron came to Cupid more than a hundred years ago, and Camerons have owned and worked the Straight Arrow Ranch—the largest spread in these parts—ever since.

For kids and kisses, tears and laughter, wild horses and wilder men—come to the Straight Arrow Ranch, near Cupid, Colorado. Come meet the Camerons.

**THE CAMERONS OF COLORADO**
by Ruth Jean Dale

**Kids, Critters and Cupid (Superromance#678)**
available in February 1996

**The Cupid Conspiracy (Temptation #579)**
available in March 1996

**The Cupid Chronicles (Superromance #687)**
available in April 1996

# You're About to Become a

## *Privileged Woman*

Reap the rewards of fabulous free gifts and benefits with proofs-of-purchase from Harlequin and Silhouette books

# Pages & Privileges™

It's our way of thanking you for buying our books at your favorite retail stores.

```
┌ ─ ─ ─ ─ ─ ─ ─ ─ ─ ─ ─ ─ ┐
│         PROOF OF        │  HT-PP103
│         PURCHASE        │
│ Offer expires October 31,1996 │
└ ─ ─ ─ ─ ─ ─ ─ ─ ─ ─ ─ ─ ┘
```

### Harlequin and Silhouette— the most privileged readers in the world!

For more information about Harlequin and Silhouette's PAGES & PRIVILEGES program call the Pages & Privileges Benefits Desk: 1-503-794-2499

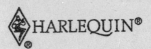

HARLEQUIN®